Happy Birthday

25 Successful Years!

Hope there are many more.

Best Wishes

Anne Mather

Dear Reader,

Reflecting on the twenty-fifth anniversary of Harlequin Presents® has led me to contemplate other milestones. It's twenty-four years since my first book was published by Mills & Boon in the U.K., and fifteen since my initial appearance in Presents. Over the years I trust my values have deepened and expanded, causing the conflicts and conversations of my characters to break new ground. Growth is one thing anniversaries commemorate—my congratulations to Harlequin for the phenomenal growth of Harlequin Presents®. May it continue!

Warmly,

Sandra Field

Sandra Field

SANDRA FIELD

Girl Trouble

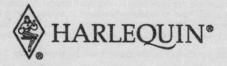

TORONTO • NEW YORK • LONDON
AMSTERDAM • PARIS • SYDNEY • HAMBURG
STOCKHOLM • ATHENS • TOKYO • MILAN • MADRID
PRAGUE • WARSAW • BUDAPEST • AUCKLAND

ISBN 0-373-11964-X

GIRL TROUBLE

First North American Publication 1998.

CHAPTER ONE

Two shocks in one day.

The first had been pleasurable, rife with possibilities and potential. The second was like a kick in the gut.

Cade MacInnis stood very still in the middle of the sidewalk of one of Halifax's busiest streets. It was a sunny day in June and he was back in Nova Scotia on vacation. He should have looked relaxed and happy. Instead, his mouth was a slash in his face and his shoulders were hunched, his fists thrust in the pockets of his jeans. He looked like he was ready to explode.

The jostling crowds on the sidewalk—it was noon and the offices had emptied—swirled around him, avoiding him, although some of the women sneaked backward glances at this tall, broad-shouldered figure with its air of pent-up emotion and physical prowess. But Cade was as oblivious to his observers as he was to the sun's rays glinting in his black, curly hair. Rather, his gaze was fastened on the large photograph framed and mounted in a glass case on the brick wall of a photographer's studio. A photograph of a woman with two children. Both girls.

Most people looking at the photo would have smiled, for all three, woman and girls, were dressed in denim dungarees, white shirts with the sleeves rolled up, and scarlet bandannas tied in jaunty bows around their necks; all three had baseball caps perched on their blond hair, and all three were clowning at the photographer, leaning on each other in casually exaggerated poses, laughing comically. The woman was clearly the mother of the two girls, for the resemblance was strong, the girls already showing the promise of a beauty possessed in abundance by their mother.

One girl, the one with the fall of straight, shiny hair, looked about nine; the other, who had an untidy tumble of curls around a heart-shaped face, was possibly five or six.

And then there was the mother.

Cade's eyes, eyes of so dark a brown as to be almost black, returned to the woman and stayed there, fastening on her as though the very intensity of his gaze could make her step from the frame, appear before him, and speak as he hadn't heard her speak for over ten years.

He'd known the instant he'd seen the photograph that it was Lorraine. Lorraine Campbell, daughter of Morris Campbell, a man wealthier than Cade ever aspired to be. Cade had fallen in love with Lorraine when she was sixteen and he twenty. Old enough to know better, he thought now. But he hadn't known better. Hadn't had the common sense of a flea.

She was Lorraine Cartwright now, of course. Wife of Ray Cartwright, businessman and entrepreneur, a man Cade had distrusted and disliked from the first time he'd met him eleven or twelve years ago.

She'd changed in ten years. The photo, he thought cynically, was no doubt touched up. But there was no disguising the new maturity in her face, the way it had fined down to an essential elegance of design: high forehead and long-lashed blue eyes over taut cheekbones and a generous curve of mouth. Her hair was different than he remembered. In its natural state, he knew, it was as straight as her elder daughter's, with the sheen and flow of river water in sunlight. In the photograph it was a tangle of bouncy curls that somehow echoed the laughter in her face. Lorraine obviously liked being Ray's wife. Ray, too, of course, was rich. Would keep her in the style to which she was accustomed, cocooned by the society in which she had grown up.

She'd always been out of reach.

Except once.

With a huge effort Cade tried to bring himself back to reality. He was making a fool of himself. Gaping at a photo as though it were alive.

Perhaps it was, he realized with a jolt. In one way. Because ever since he'd seen it, every cell in his body had become a roil of emotion, every muscle a tightly coiled spring. Anger, hatred, humiliation, helplessness, despair...the list was endless and he felt them all. He could have been twenty-three again, the intervening years vanished as if they'd never been.

By the time he was twenty-three everything had fallen apart. That was the year she'd married Ray.

Then, like another hard kick to the gut, he finally admitted something else, something he'd been doing his damnedest to avoid. He'd left out one emotion on the list. Omitted it purposely. And no wonder, because it was the most powerful of them all. Desire. A raging and all-consuming desire. For even in baggy overalls with scarlet sneakers on her feet and a silly cap on her head, Lorraine Cartwright was utterly and irresistibly desirable.

As she had been ever since she'd turned sixteen and he'd seen her in her very first evening gown standing in the moonlight. She'd looked so young and beautiful, so touchingly vulnerable, that Cade had for the first time in his life understood what those overused words "falling in love" meant. For it was as though he had indeed fallen, a vast, swooping descent into a mystical place he'd never known existed, a place illuminated by her very existence, a place where he would have done anything in the world for her. A place where—at first—he'd been content to worship from afar.

Furious with himself, Cade tamped down a flood of memories that, if he ever gave them place, could drown him. He hated her. Had hated her for years, and with good reason. He'd do well to remember that.

Love was an emotion long gone; it was no longer on the list. She'd killed it. Cruelly and deliberately, in a way he'd never forgotten or forgiven.

Stop it! he berated himself. For God's sake, quit while you're still ahead. It's only a photograph, a piece of colored paper stuck in a gold frame. A printed image of a woman who's as inaccessible now as she ever was, and not worth the time you're wasting on her. That's all it is. Nothing more.

You've got more important things to do than stand on the sidewalk as if you've been hit on the head and don't know which way is up. Like think about Sam's offer. Like get some lunch.

He strode around the corner and pushed open the door to the photography studio.

It was cool inside, the decor an attractive blend of glossy-leafed plants and cleverly arranged portraits. The middle-aged woman behind the counter gave him a friendly smile. "Can I help you, sir?"

Cade should have smiled back; but his face felt as stiff as a board. "There's a photo in your showcase outside," he said abruptly. "Of a woman with her two daughters."

"Oh, yes…it turned out rather well, didn't it?"

"I—I knew her years ago. But we've gotten out of touch. I wondered—does she live around here?"

The woman's smile became a little guarded. "I'm very sorry, sir, I can't really give you any details. We—"

"Her name's Lorraine. Lorraine Cartwright. I used to work for her father, Morris Campbell."

"We have a policy of client confidentiality, as I'm

sure you understand," the woman said. "Is there any other way I can be of assistance to you?"

Leave, Cade, he thought. Get out of here. Now. You're making a total ass of yourself. "Can I get a copy of the photo?" he said hoarsely.

The woman was now regarding him through narrowed eyes. "That wouldn't be possible without the express permission of my client," she said briskly. "And now, if you'll excuse me, sir?"

Cade turned on his heel and left the studio. Without giving the showcase a second look he marched down the street, blind to the tourists, office workers, students and children who thronged the pavement. Good work, MacInnis, he jeered. That woman in the studio—a thoroughly nice woman by the look of her—now thinks you're a combination of a weirdo, a psychotic and a stalker.

You're none of the above. But you're an idiot. Letting Lorraine Cartwright jerk you around as if you were thirteen, not thirty-three pushing thirty-four. Grow up, will you? Quit reliving a fairy tale.

For hadn't that whole three years between twenty and twenty-three had the remoteness, the otherwordly air of "once upon a time"? Lorraine, with her long blond hair and her cool blue eyes, had been cast as the princess, who one night in a fit of pique had thrown herself at Cade the commoner, the peasant, the tall, dark and—so he'd been told—handsome young worker on her father's estate. Manfully the commoner had refused to take advantage of the princess's youth, beauty, and undoubted virginity. Had the princess very prettily thanked the commoner? Had she presented him with a silk scarf she'd embroidered with her own fair hands as a memento of his noble act of abstention? No, indeed. She'd turned on him like a virago and then she'd engineered that her father fire Cade from his job.

Nor, he thought bitterly, had the peasant ever turned into a prince.

Unfortunately the story hadn't ended there; and the rest of it was more difficult to fit into the mode of fairy tale. For someone from the village had seen him and Lorraine in the woods that evening, had witnessed their initial, impassioned embrace, and gossip had spread like wildfire through the little village of Juniper Hills. Cade had fought several pitched battles on Lorraine's behalf, defending her virtue like a true knight of old. At which point three hired thugs—paid for by Lorraine's father, spurred on by Lorraine—had given Cade the beating of his lifetime. Afterward Lorraine had made a point of calling at the garage where he worked, where she'd let him know with humiliating accuracy how little his militancy on her behalf was appreciated.

That scene was still seared in Cade's memory. It had been, he supposed, the worst moment of his life. Worse by far than the beating, and that had been bad enough for a young fellow who'd prided himself on his fists.

Somehow Cade's feet had carried him all the way down to the waterfront. A fish and chips truck was parked outside the market. But his appetite had disappeared and he was in no mood to stand patiently in the lineup and wait for his turn.

He'd go back to the hotel, change into his running gear and head for the park. He had to do something physical, and soon. Or else he'd go nuts.

Twenty-five minutes later Cade was jogging under the tall pines of Point Pleasant Park, which was situated on a peninsula jutting into the waters of Halifax Harbour and which had as its view the knife-sharp edge where the open Atlantic met the sky. He passed the container pier and the war monument, feeling his muscles loosen and his stride settle into an easy rhythm. Lorraine was nothing to him. Nothing.

Quite apart from anything else, she was a married woman. Happily married, by the look of her.

Which, considering the man she'd chosen for a husband, didn't say much for her.

He forced himself to put her out of his mind, to concentrate on his surroundings. A group of children were playing ball on the grass by the edge of the harbor, their cries like the chittering of sparrows; dogs chased each other through the trees, and other joggers passed him, some breathing easily, some gasping for air. He ran through the woodland trails for the better part of an hour, then stretched out his calves against a tree and found himself a perch on the weathered rocks that overlooked the Northwest Arm. It was time, he thought wryly, wiping the sweat from his brow with the hem of his T-shirt, to think about shock number one. The one that Sam had landed on him when they'd met for breakfast that morning in the little diner across from Sam's garage.

Sam Withrod. He'd been the area supervisor for a chain of gas stations, one of which had been leased to Cade's father in the years when Cade had been growing up. Cade had always liked Sam. Liked him and respected him. They'd kept in touch ever since, one or two letters a year, short letters on Cade's part, long newsy letters on Sam's. When he'd come back to Canada a year ago and taken the job in Toronto, Cade had phoned Sam, and somehow they'd fallen into a pattern of monthly phone calls.

This morning Sam had offered Cade a job. More than a job. A partnership in his business.

"I'm sixty-four years old," Sam had said, plastering his toast with butter. "Got no kin, no sons of my own. Not as bright-eyed and busy-tailed as I used to be, either. I'd like it just fine if you'd take over the garage eventually, Cade. When I get ready to retire. In the meantime I'd like you to be a full partner, learn the business, give me your ideas and your input. What d'you say?''

Sam specialized in foreign cars, employed a dozen mechanics and had always had an impeccable reputation for efficiency and honesty. Cade said blankly, ''Do you mean it?''

''Sure do. Hadn't you seen it coming?''

''Can't say I had.''

''You're not that happy in Toronto.''

''Hate it,'' Cade said economically. ''The city and the job. You can't get out of the city and the job's going nowhere.''

Sam gulped down the last of his bacon and eggs and swiped at his mustache with his serviette; his mustache, like his hair, was thick, white and bushy. ''You're in town for a few days. Come see me at the garage, look around, ask questions. Then think it over and let me know. No rush.''

Playing with his fork, Cade said awkwardly, ''It's a very generous offer, Sam.''

''I don't think so,'' Sam said, his bright blue eyes both shrewd and affectionate. ''I watched you grow up, boy. You work like a demon and you've got a way with an engine like some men have with a woman. But most of all, you're loyal and you're trustworthy...I'd take your word to the bank any day of the week. And I can't say that for too many folks I meet.''

Cade, moved, had said gruffly, ''Thanks,'' had quickly signaled to the waitress for more coffee and had changed the subject. But now, as he sat alone watching the sun dance on the water, he could allow Sam's words to play through him, warming him inside as the sun was warming his skin. Sam trusted him. That was the gist of it.

Excitement kindled within him. He'd be willing to bet

that Sam's business was flourishing; foreign cars were becoming more and more popular, and in a city as small as Halifax the word would get around that the garage was honest in its dealings. Already in Toronto Cade had gotten himself into hot water because of his refusal to condone shoddy or unnecessary work; and the boss's son was waiting in the sidelines to take over just as soon as his father gave the word.

He, Cade, could live by the sea again, in a province known for its shoreline and its wilderness, places where a man could stretch his legs and breathe free. Nor would he continually have to be shoving his principles down his boss's throat; because Sam shared those principles. He could be closer to his mother, too; she still lived in Juniper Hills, a forty-minute drive from Halifax.

Closer to Lorraine? That, too?

Scowling, Cade stared at the far shore. Now that a couple of hours had passed since his impetuous entrance to the photography studio and his ignominious exit, he was appalled by how deeply the sight of that photograph had affected him. In taking him by surprise, it had revealed something about himself that he would have preferred not to know. That he was no more free of Lorraine now than he had been ten years ago.

Not that he'd spent the ten years constantly thinking about her. Far from it. He'd left Juniper Hills before he turned twenty-four, right after his father died. He'd roamed the rest of Canada, then the States, Chile, Australia, Thailand and Singapore, India and Turkey, ending up in Europe and finally Great Britain. He'd worked at everything from sheep ranching to dishwashing, he'd read voraciously, studied whenever he'd had the chance, and in terms of visas had stayed—more or less—one step ahead of the law. He'd grown up. Or so he'd thought until an hour ago.

For the first time it occurred to him to wonder if it

perhaps hadn't been the smartest of moves to bury in the depths of his unconscious everything that had happened with Lorraine so long ago. Because it had all lain there waiting for him, a bundle of dynamite with a coiled fuse; to which, today, that damned photograph had touched the blue flame of a match.

Cade's mind made a sudden leap. Maybe Lorraine was the reason he'd never married. Although he hadn't been celibate in the last ten years, he'd confined his occasional affairs to women for whom he'd felt a certain affection, yet who'd clearly understood that commitment wasn't on his agenda: he'd be moving on as soon as his visa ran out. Moving on by himself. Trouble was, some of those women would happily have marched him up the aisle to the stately strains of Mendelssohn. Which had always made him feel as skittish as a fox kit and twice as wary.

Because he'd never really freed himself from Lorraine? From all the tangled emotions that had bound him to her? Was she his albatross, the weight who kept him from flying free?

Or was he, quite simply, a loner? A man who'd always felt most comfortable in his own company, free to follow his own instincts wherever they led him? In essence, ever since he'd started school he'd been on his own, fighting one battle after another in defense of his father in the school grounds: fights that at first he lost consistently. He could remember as easily as if it were yesterday the Martin brothers, who'd found it roaringly funny to lurch up and down outside the school library imitating the drunken staggers of Cade's father. No one had ever come to Cade's help when the Martin boys had pinned him to the ground and pummeled him until—sometimes—he'd cried. He must have realized way back then that he was on his own, alone in a world often hostile. Certainly he couldn't have run home for solace from his mother.

So perhaps Lorraine had nothing whatsoever to do with his unmarried state.

She'd looked so goddamned happy in that photograph! So carefree. Yet her husband, unless all Cade's radar had been way off base, was a sleaze.

A rich sleaze, though. A high-society sleaze. Not like himself, plain Cade MacInnis, whose dad used to run the local gas station. And Lorraine, as a teenager, had been a crashing snob. Why should she have changed?

Cade surged to his feet. Enough. This afternoon he'd go to Sam's garage, and then he'd make his decision. Unless it was already made. Was he was going to move back to Nova Scotia to live by the sea? And then do his best to engineer a meeting between himself and Lorraine Cartwright, so that once and for all he could lay that particular ghost to rest? He didn't want his emotional life on permanent hold because of her; nor did he want her lodged so deeply in his being that the sight of a photograph knocked him right off balance.

His mother probably knew where Lorraine and Ray were living. He'd ask her, track Lorraine down that way.

It's a plan, he thought savagely. Yeah, it's a plan. Because it's time I get on with my life. Alone or not. If I have to see Lorraine Cartwright once more in order to leave the past where it belongs—nicely in the past, thank you very much—then that's what I'll do.

A good old-fashioned exorcism, that's what I need.

Because I hate like hell feeling tied to that woman. In any way at all. She's not worth the time of day, and never was.

CHAPTER TWO

THREE months later, on a Saturday morning in September as sunny and warm as that morning in June had been, Cade pushed open the door to the gymnasium of one of Halifax's universities. Just yesterday he'd joined as an off-campus member. He'd been so busy the last few weeks settling into his new job as Sam's partner and into his apartment, not to mention buying the property at French Bay, that he'd been neglecting his usual fitness routine. Past time to get himself in better shape.

He spent three-quarters of an hour in the weight room going through his regular routine. Although he didn't overdo the weights, Cade felt much better for the exercise.

Once he'd showered, he'd go to French Bay to check out what the carpenter and plumber had accomplished in the last couple of days. His purchase four weeks ago of ten acres and a rundown house on the shores of a bay only twenty minutes outside the city had been uncharacteristically impulsive. Yet Cade knew in his bones it had been the right decision; just as coming back to Halifax and taking Sam's offer of a partnership had been. After his many years of wandering, he'd come home.

As he left the weight room, a woman's voice suddenly overrode the chatter of the students who were lounging in the corridor waiting for a class to begin. "I'll be right there," the voice called. "Just let me get the tapes."

Cade's head swiveled around. All the hairs lifted on the back of his neck. Lorraine. That voice belonged to Lorraine. He'd swear it did.

But it couldn't be her. What would she be doing in a crowded university gym on a Saturday morning? He was out of his mind to even think it was her. He hadn't seen her for years, and lots of other women must be gifted with attractive contralto voices that had that edge of throatiness he recalled so well.

He turned and strode down the hallway toward the voice, went around the corner and collided head-on with its owner.

It *was* Lorraine.

Cade's heart gave a great thud, as though he'd dropped a 20-kilogram weight on the carpet. Automatically his arms went around her, steadying her. In one startled and all-comprehensive moment he saw that she was both totally different and absolutely the same.

Her hair, which used to be a sleek, polished fall curving around her cheeks, was now pulled back into a ponytail with wisps curling over her eyes. But it was the same warm blond, streaked from the sun. Her eyes—blank now with shock—were the smudged blue he remembered, a blue the color of kingfisher feathers. She looked tired; the shadows under her eyes were tinged a translucent shade somewhere between blue and mauve.

Her fingers, lying against the chest of his sweat-damp singlet, were slim and strong. But Lorraine at nineteen had had nails painted all shades from scarlet to garish pink; her nails were now bare of polish. Her hands were bare of rings, too, he saw with a ripple along his nerves.

The gentle curve of her belly was pressed against him, and as he looked down at her he was rewarded by an enticing and altogether disturbing view of her cleavage. Her breasts were fuller than they used to be, he thought, his mouth dry.

"*Cade!*" she gasped. "Cade MacInnis...what are *you* doing here?"

More details thrust their way into Cade's addled brain. She was wearing an aerobics outfit, a shiny neon-pink latex top whose brevity made his head swim, and equally close-fitting black shorts. Her hips were deliciously rounded. To his horror he felt his groin begin to stiffen.

Her eyes widened and her cheeks flooded with color. Roughly Cade pushed her away, infuriated by his body's betrayal, even more angry that she should be aware of it. He said harshly, "Lifting weights. What about you?"

"I—I have an aerobics class. But what are you doing in the city? I thought you were in Australia. Or Chile, or somewhere."

"Australia was seven years ago, Chile eight." Realizing he was still clasping her by the shoulders, bare except for the straps of her top, he let his hands fall and bent to pick up the towel he'd dropped when she'd bumped into him. "I live here now," he said.

"*Live* here? Since when?"

"A couple of months ago. You don't look very pleased."

That was putting it mildly. She looked appalled, distraught, even—his eyes narrowed—frightened. Now why should the reappearance of a man she'd spurned many years ago—had treated like dirt—make a woman as self-possessed as Lorraine Cartwright afraid?

She pushed a strand of hair back from her face; her fingers were trembling very slightly. Making an obvious effort to gather her wits, she said, "It's nothing to me where you live, of course. It just startled me, that's all, seeing you after all these years."

"Ten," Cade said. "Remember? The last time we talked was at the gas station in August."

Two days after the beating. He watched her pale, then flush an unbecoming shade of red. "I suppose so. Look, I've got to—"

"So have you become a student in your old age, Lorraine?" he asked with an unpleasant smile.

Her chin tilted. "Lori," she said. "I go by Lori now."

It wasn't the answer he'd expected. "Lori...why the change of name?"

Her chin went a little higher. "Why not?"

In other words, mind your own business, Cade MacInnis. Oddly, he thought the abbreviated name suited her. Lorraine went with the disdainful air of that much younger woman, the one with smooth hair and polished fingernails. The one way she hadn't looked so far today was disdainful. "You didn't answer my question," he said.

He could see her searching her memory. "Oh...oh, no, I'm not a student."

A blond guy over six feet tall and built like a football player punched her lightly on the arm with a familiarity that raised Cade's hackles. "Hey, Lori—you ready to go?"

"I'll be right there, Tory. Cade, I have to go, I've got a class. It's been...nice to see you again."

"Nice? Tell the truth, Lori, you'd rather I was in Patagonia. How's Ray?"

She flashed him a look he could only describe as hunted, mumbled, "'Bye," and, joined by a crowd of students, headed for the large room where aerobics classes were held.

Cade stayed where he was, his eyes glued to the blond ponytail of the woman he had once loved with all the desperation of youth, and then had hated equally fiercely and with youth's complete lack of compromise. *Nice to see you...* Who are you kidding, Lorraine Cartwright? Patagonia's too close for your liking. Central Antarctica would suit you better.

She was no more indifferent to him than he to her. That much he'd learned from a conversation as baffling as it had been brief. That, and the fact that for some reason his sudden appearance had frightened her.

He strolled over to the ceiling-high windows that bordered one side of the aerobics room. The music had already started, poundingly loud, with an accelerated rock beat that was one of the reasons he'd never ventured near an aerobics class. Then his fist tightened on his towel. Lori was perched on a raised dais at the front of the room, doing toe taps and arm raises as the beginning of a warm-up. She wasn't a member of the class. She was teaching it.

Lorraine Cartwright teaching an aerobics class to a bunch of students? What the hell was going on? The Lorraine he knew might have been riding her thoroughbred horse, or shopping in Montreal, or going to plays and concerts in New York. But she wouldn't have been teaching aerobics.

The class was mixed, male and female, with a preponderance of students in bright garb, but also with some older people in the back rows, even a gray head or two. The student called Tory was in the front row, enthusiastically jabbing his fists over his head. Cade stepped closer, watching Lori as she started marching on the spot. Her breasts bounced as she moved. The smooth play of muscles in her arms and legs bewitched him. Oh great, he thought caustically. A cold shower, that's what you need, and saw her glance in his direction. Her step faltered, losing the beat.

Too bad I'm not in Patagonia, isn't it, Lori? Too bad I'm right here in Halifax. Because you and I have some unfinished business, and I'm going to make damn sure we deal with it.

Almost as if she could read his thoughts, she hurriedly looked away, picking up the rhythm again. Cade had had enough of watching her. He shouldered his towel and headed for the showers.

When he emerged, wearing jeans and a summer shirt, his hair in wet curls on his scalp, the class was still in progress. Everyone was jogging on the spot, doing arm raises at a fast clip; Lori looked as cool and energetic as she had twenty minutes ago. She did not look his way.

Cade strolled to the front desk and picked up an aerobics schedule. She was listed as L. Cartwright. She taught six days a week. He frowned at the neatly typed list, wondering why Lorraine, who had never lacked for anything in her life, was teaching six classes a week for, probably, not much more than minimum wage. Thoughtfully he folded the schedule and put it in his kit bag. Then he said to the young woman who was handing out towels, "I have a pass for the weight room. Next week could I try out a couple of aerobics classes to see if I'd like to add that to my membership?"

"No problem," she said. "Just pick up a guest pass on your way in."

Monday he'd take early lunch at the garage, come to Lori's class and then corner her afterward. After all, the two of them had quite a bit to talk about. He wanted to confront her with her actions of ten years ago. He also wanted to know what was going on in her life right now. She owed him a few answers, did Lori Cartwright. And maybe when he'd gotten them, he'd get over this adolescent obsession with her.

He'd better. What other options did he have?

As Cade turned away, fumbling for his car keys in his pocket, he noticed for the first time the two little girls who were sitting in padded green chairs by the doorway to the gym. Both were blond, one with straight hair and one with curly. Lori's daughters, he thought with a lurch of his gut. They were squabbling, the elder girl giving officious directions, the younger whining in a manner calculated to aggravate.

Cade took a deep breath and walked over to them.

"Hello," he said pleasantly. "My name's Cade. Your mother and I were friends years ago, before she was married. What are your names?"

The younger one crowed, "We're not supposed to talk to strangers. Come *on*, Rachel, give it to me." She made a grab for her sister's hand.

Rachel pulled back. "Stop it, Liddy, you're being a brat and I'm going to tell Mum how bad you were."

"I'll tell her you wouldn't give me my gum. 'Cause you're so mean and horrible." Liddy's face crumpled with maximum histrionic effect. "I'm only little, you shouldn't be so awful to me."

With matching melodrama Rachel cast her eyes heavenward—kingfisher-blue eyes, Cade noticed with a catch at his heart—and said, "You're the one's who's horrible. Take your silly gum, see if I care."

Liddy snatched at the package and jammed a huge wad of bright pink gum into her mouth. "I bet I can make a bigger bubble than you," she announced triumphantly.

"Oh yeah?" said Rachel, and blew a marvelously stretched bubble that, miraculously, didn't end up smeared all over her face.

Cade said, casually he hoped, "Is your dad coming to get you?"

The gum was forgotten. Rachel and Liddy both directed stares of uniform hostility at him and said nothing. Cade had never thought of himself as easily frightened, but there was something about their instant alliance and the cold blue of their gaze that disconcerted him. He said, determined not to be outstared, "I guess I shouldn't have asked that, I'm sorry. I hope I'll see you both again." Then he pushed open the swing door and stepped outside into the sunshine.

They won that round, he thought ruefully. Hands down. And why should he be surprised that Lori's daughters had strong personalities? Lori had never been what you'd call backward.

But Lori wasn't going to win the next round. The one that was slated for Monday at noon.

At five to twelve on Monday, Cade wandered into the aerobics room at the gym. Two or three others were already there, chatting desultorily at the front of the room. Lori was kneeling in the back corner, putting her tapes into the machine. Soundlessly he walked up behind her. "Good morning," he said. "Or is it good afternoon?"

Her whole body jerked, then went still. With a deliberation he had to admire, she finished adjusting the controls on the tape deck before she looked around. Her eyes skidded up his long, well-muscled legs, his shorts and loose singlet. Quickly she pushed herself to her feet. "Good morning, Cade," she said. "The weight room's two doors down. Or had you forgotten?"

"Unfortunately, I forget very little." He held out his guest pass. "Thought I'd try aerobics today. One should always be open to new experiences, don't you agree?"

"You're coming to my class?" she said tightly.

"That's the plan."

She looked as though any number of sizzling retorts were on the tip of her tongue. He watched her swallow them as four more people came through the door. "Fine," she snapped. "Just don't overdo it your first day, I'd hate to see you hurt yourself."

"Come off it, Lori," he said softly. "You'd like to see me carried out on a stretcher."

"No, I wouldn't, it would ruin my reputation as a teacher," she said with a sweet and patently insincere smile. "Enjoy, as they say."

He watched her walk away. Today her top was green, her shorts navy. Both were shiny and both clung to all the right places. She didn't look like the mother of two children. Cade positioned himself in the back row and prepared to pay attention.

A considerable number of people had gathered in the room by now. At the last minute a middle-aged woman rushed in the door and headed for the back row. Inwardly Cade flinched; it was the woman from the studio, the one where he'd seen the photo of Lori and her two daughters. The woman caught sight of him, gave him a pungent glance liberally dosed with suspicion, and pointedly moved forward a row. This, at any other time, might have amused Cade.

The class began. Very soon Cade concluded that Lori was very good at her job, no matter what her reasons were for having it. She referred to people by name, she kept up a running stream of encouragement and banter, and she insisted on good technique. The sequence of moves was extremely vigorous, disabusing him of any notions that aerobics was for sissies. The others in the class were accustomed to these moves; Cade was not. More than once he found his arms and legs at odds not only with each other but also with the smoothly orchestrated steps everyone else was taking. Including the big blond student called Tory, stationed once more in the very front row. He, Cade, had been smart to stay in the back, he thought irritably.

He found himself sidestepping to the left and doing bicep curls while the rest were stepping to the right and had switched to a rapid overhead move Lori was calling the arrowhead. Wishing he had half his father's coordination—for Dan MacInnis had been an inventive dancer—Cade struggled on. It wasn't the moment for Lori to look down at him, give him another sweet smile and say in a carrying voice, "Get your legs doing the moves first. The arms can follow. And you can always march on the spot if this is too strenuous."

If sweat hadn't been dripping into his eyes—he hadn't worn his sweatband figuring he wouldn't need it for a mere aerobics class—and if he hadn't been determined to accomplish what students who were roughly half his age were doing with ease, Cade might have thought of a witty retort.

Just as he was getting the hang of what she was up to, Lori switched to something called the grapevine. "Keep your hips angled forward, not sideways...like this," she called out. Cade looked at her hips, at their supple movements and delectable roundness, and stumbled out of step again.

He thoroughly disliked feeling like an uncoordinated klutz, he who rather prided himself on his body's fitness. He scowled at Lori as his arms alternated triceps and lateral raises, thinking meanly, I bet you can't bench press 250 pounds, lady.

Pretty childish. About Liddy's level. Even if it does make you feel better.

She was jogging now, jogging as lightly as if she had springs in her heels, carrying the class along on her own energy and cajoling them in a way they plainly loved. This was not the woman he remembered. She wouldn't have lowered herself to such a mundane task, let alone enjoyed it.

Some of the stretches in the last ten minutes used muscles Cade hadn't even known existed; by the time the class ended, his hair was clinging wetly to his scalp and he was in dire need of a shower.

As Lori ran to the back of the room to get her tapes, he walked over to her. There were patches of sweat on her green top both down her spine and under her breasts; he thought they were one of the most erotic things he'd ever seen. He said truthfully, "I sure know I've been exercising. You run a good class—thanks."

"It's my job," she said dismissively.

"Got time for a coffee? Or a sandwich in the cafeteria?"

"No. Thanks."

It was time to make his move, the one he'd rehearsed on the way over. "Lori," Cade said, taking her by the elbow as she would have walked past him, "it must be as obvious to you as it is to me that you and I need to have a talk."

Her lashes flickered. She said in a rush, "I have only one thing to say, Cade...although it is important. I'm truly sorry that all those years ago I was partially responsible for getting you fired. Truly sorry. Now let go of me, please."

"Partially?" he flashed. "That's not the way I see it."

"Partially. That's what I said."

"Let's not get hung up on semantics—you got me fired."

"It was more complicated than that."

"It was very simple. You told Daddy and Daddy fired me."

"How very convenient for you that rich rhymes with bitch!" Refusing to drop her gaze, Lori yanked at her arm. "Let go! Because that's it. There's nothing else we could possibly need to discuss."

He said in a level voice, "Why did you look so frightened the first time you saw me?"

"Cade," Lori said, "the past is the past. Dead, gone and buried. I've never believed in reincarnation and I'm not going to start now. I don't want you talking to me. I don't want you talking to my children. Have you got that straight?"

"I probably shouldn't have said anything to Rachel and Liddy...I apologize for that."

"I don't see how you knew who they were."

"Come off it—they look enough like you to be clones. Plus I saw a photo of the three of you in the window of a studio downtown. The woman who owns it was in the class this morning.''

"You mean Sally put that photo on display? I'll have her hide for that!''

Cade didn't want to talk about Sally. "Just answer me one question. Why are you working at a low-paying job that must get monotonous as all get-out, as well as being hard on the body, when you've got a rich husband and a very rich father?''

With a touch of her old haughtiness she ignored his question. "Take a hint, will you?'' she retorted. "I have nothing to say to you. Not one word. If you persist in harassing me like this, I'll lay a complaint and have you barred from the class.''

"For all your faults, you were never a coward,'' he drawled, and decided the time had come to fight dirty. "Do you remember the night you threw yourself at me, Lorraine? Or have you conveniently buried that memory along with another one—the way you spoke to me at the gas pumps in August? Remember? I had a black eye, three fractured ribs and two broken fingers.''

For a moment her teeth clamped themselves to her lower lip. Her infinitely kissable lip, thought Cade, and wondered if he'd thrown away any chance of her ever speaking to him again. He hadn't liked her using the word harass. Hadn't liked it one bit.

"There's no point in this!'' she cried. "I hate rummaging through the past, hauling stuff up that's better left buried. We went our separate ways all those years ago—and that's the way it still is.''

Abruptly he dropped her elbow and held out his hands; he was never fully able to remove the traces of grease ingrained in the creases of his skin from his work at the garage, and his knuckles were marred by scars and scratches. "I'm still not good enough for you, am I?'' he grated. "I'm just a mechanic. A grease monkey. So far below you that you won't even have a coffee with me in the university cafeteria."

"That's not—" Her eyes widened and her fingers, light as falling leaves, rested on his wrist. "Cade, what happened there?"

A jagged white scar ran from the back of his left hand to the inside of his wrist. He stared down at her fingers, feeling their warmth burn his flesh, and said flatly, "Accident on an oil rig in the North Sea. A couple of years ago. What do you care, Lori?"

She dropped her hand to her side and took a deep breath. Then she said quietly, "We've both got scars, haven't we? Some outside and some in. That's what living does to you. Please listen to me—I don't want to hurt you and I certainly don't look down on you. But you and I have nothing more to say to each other. You must accept that and leave me alone."

"And where are your scars?"

"Cade...please."

He'd always loved the shade of her irises, a color that hovered somewhere between blue and green, reminding him of the shimmering reflections along a lakeshore on a summer's day. Right now those irises were full of appeal. He said nastily, "Very touching. You've learned a trick or two since I last knew you."

She whispered, "You hate me, don't you?"

"Now you're beginning to get it. Can you give me any reason why I shouldn't?"

Her face hardened. "I can't give you anything," she said, each word as brittle as a shard of ice.

"Ray always struck me as the kind of guy who'd be insanely jealous. Is it him you're afraid of? That somehow he'll find out you and I have met up again?"

An indecipherable expression crossed her features. "I'm a married woman," she said, "that's one—"

"Why aren't you wearing your rings?"

"Here?" she said ironically. "The famous Cartwright diamonds? I don't think so."

Any stray thoughts Cade might have entertained that perhaps she and Ray had divorced in the last ten years—didn't one out of three marriages end in divorce?—were squashed. Not that it made much difference. The turmoil of emotion lodged somewhere between his stomach and his heart had very little to do with Ray and everything to do with Lori. What he wanted to do was take her in his arms and kiss her senseless. Ray or no Ray. Married or not. Which was scarcely the way to behave with a woman who'd just accused him, more or less accurately, of hating her.

Nor did he have the slightest idea what to say next. Because nothing had gone the way he'd rehearsed it.

She solved his dilemma for him. "I have to get home," she said coldly. "Goodbye, Cade."

His voice seemed to be trapped in his throat. He watched her leave, the graceful swing of her hips in her snug-fitting shorts, the proud carriage of her head. Not until the door swung shut behind her did Cade, finally, work out exactly what it was he was feeling. It wasn't hatred. It wasn't anger. Nothing so simple. It was pain. Outright, all-encompassing pain. Lori Cartwright wanted no more to do with him now than had Lorraine Campbell all those years ago.

Pain? Because a woman he despised was rejecting him? He was losing his mind.

More to the point, what was he going to do about it?

Cade was no nearer an answer to this question by the time he got back to the garage, had shrugged into his overalls and addressed himself to the intricate workings of a custom-built Mercedes. Sam had been checking the idling speed on a Volkswagen Passat that one of the apprentices was working on; he wandered over to Cade and said offhandedly, "Good lunch?"

Cade chose a different wrench and made an indeterminate sound that could have meant anything.

"What did you have?"

"What?"

"To eat," Sam said patiently.

"Nothing. I forgot. To eat, I mean. I went to the gym."

"You okay, boy?"

No, thought Cade. I'm not okay. I've got a lump in the pit of my stomach as big as the battery in this car and all I can think about is a woman with kingfisher-blue eyes and a body to die for. A body I lust after. Me, who's managed to keep my sexuality very much under control for years. "I'm fine," he said. "You want to go over those accounts after we close?"

"You don't have to lie to me," Sam said mildly. "Just tell me to butt out."

Finally Cade looked up. "Sam, I'm sorry," he said. "It's woman troubles, okay?"

"Didn't take you long...what is it, less than three months since you moved here? Not that I'm surprised. You always did attract the women."

All except for one. "I don't want to talk about it," Cade said through gritted teeth.

"Nothing new about that—you never were much of a one for talk." Sam grinned at him. "We'll go for a bite to eat once we close and we'll do the accounts after that. No point starving yourself for the sake of true love. The manual for the Mercedes is in the office if you need it." Smiling benignly, Sam sauntered off.

True love. Huh, thought Cade. What he felt for Lori was nothing to do with love. Lust, definitely. Frustration beyond anything he'd ever experienced. A rage that frightened him with its force. But not love. No, sir.

Thoroughly exasperated with himself for parading his emotions so blatantly that Sam had picked up there was something wrong, Cade went to get the manual. He'd figured out one thing today. His neat little theory that once he'd seen Lorraine he'd be able to get on with his life had been shot down in flames at high noon. Instead of exorcising her—had he actually used that word to himself? How naive could you get?—he'd only gotten in deeper.

But he'd never in his life been involved with a married woman and he wasn't going to start now. Not that Lorraine wanted anything to do with him. So his high-minded principles weren't worth a heck of a lot.

Some days, Cade decided morosely, scanning the crowded shelf of manuals, you just plain shouldn't get out of bed.

CHAPTER THREE

THAT evening Cade phoned his mother. Nina MacInnis was a schoolteacher who'd managed for years to instill a love of learning into adolescents more interested in the opposite sex than in modern literature. Although her husband Dan, Cade's father, had been an accomplished dancer and a man of great charm, he'd also been an alcoholic who several times a year would drink himself into insensibility. This Nina had suffered in silence, a silence that would ring with things unsaid and had made the young Cade long for shouting matches and thrown plates; they'd have been easier to deal with.

Two years ago she'd arranged for early retirement and had taken up with the school principal, a widower who never touched alcohol, who had an endearing sense of humor and who loved to travel. Cade, on his first visit a couple of months ago, had been delighted by the change in his mother and had liked the principal enormously. So the first thing he said when Nina picked up the phone was, "I thought you and Wilbur might have left for Outer Mongolia."

"He's in the living room watching the hockey game and having a cup of tea," said Nina primly. "But we're thinking of flying to Hawaii before Christmas."

"Go for it, Mum. And say hello to him for me." Cade went on to chat about other things, describing the new deck that had been built on the front of his house in French Bay, and asking her advice on colors for the bathroom. Then he said, rather mendaciously, "I saw someone the other day who reminded me of Ray

Cartwright. Do you know if he and Lorraine live in Halifax?''

"I don't think so. Shortly after they got married they moved to Toronto. As far as I know, that's where they still are." Nina sniffed. "He wasn't someone you'd want to invite for tea. And I'd always hoped you'd forgotten her."

I wish I had.

For a horrible moment Cade thought he'd spoken the words out loud. He said, even more mendaciously, "I have, of course... If I put dark green tiles on the kitchen floor, what shade of paint should I go for?''

Nina gave this her serious consideration and the subject of Lorraine was dropped. After accepting an invitation to Sunday dinner, Cade put down the receiver and took out the phone book. There were two L. Cartwrights listed, no Ray Cartwright, and the only R. Cartwright lived in an area of town Ray wouldn't be seen dead in.

What was he playing about at? Even if he dialed both L. Cartwrights and one of them was Lori, she wouldn't speak to him. She'd made that all too clear today.

He remembered the look of appeal she'd given him, the huskiness in her voice when she'd pleaded with him to leave her alone. He'd sneered at her, accused her of manipulation. But what if he'd been wrong? What if her appeal had been genuine? Was Ray the reason she was so frightened? And what were the scars she'd referred to?

She hadn't made that up. He'd swear to it.

Did Ray mistreat her?

Lori was five-foot-eight, fit and agile. But she'd be no match for Ray, who'd always been a heavy man, only a couple of inches shorter than Cade's six-feet-two. To think of Ray grabbing at Lori, forcing himself on her, made Cade feel sick. He closed his eyes, a murderous rage almost choking him. I'll kill the bastard if that's what's going on. Kill him and ask questions afterward.

Right, Cade, he thought savagely. That'd really simplify Lori's life. If she's afraid of Ray, the best thing you can do is keep your distance. Just as she requested. Don't talk to her. Don't go near the gym at the times of her classes. Stay away from her kids. And quit mooning over the phone book as if you're a lovesick teenager. You turned thirty-four last month and it's time you let go of the past.

Alone is the way you've operated for years. Stick with it.

He jammed the book back in the drawer and slammed it shut. That's exactly what he'd do. Let go of her. Stay away from her. Forget about her. Maybe even date other women. That way he might get lucky and get laid.

Miguel, the mechanic at the garage who specialized in Hondas, had a sister who loved movies. Cade liked movies, too. He'd ask Miguel's sister to go with him when *The English Patient* opened next week. That's what he'd do.

It would beat sitting around his apartment worrying about Lori Cartwright and proving the old adage that you always wanted what you couldn't have. He was going to prove that adage wrong. Even if he had to date twenty different women until he found one who was interested in him but not the slightest bit interested in wedding rings.

He picked up his book, the novel that had won the Booker Prize last year, and determinedly began to read.

There was nothing wrong with Cade's self-imposed advice to stay away from Lori. It was an admirable stance and should have solved all his problems. Except that twice in the next week he saw her, each time by accident. And each time stirred him up in ways that made his advice meaningless.

His apartment was in the north end of Halifax, only four or five blocks from the garage. The north end wasn't the fashionable part of the city; but Cade liked his apartment, which took up the whole second floor of an older house, had a fireplace and hardwood floors and spacious rooms with interesting nooks and crannies. And he enjoyed the walk to work each morning, finding that by now he was chatting with the old fellow who owned the corner store, and saying hello to people he passed every day on the street. It gave him a feeling of belonging; he hoped he'd find the same thing true of French Bay when he moved out there.

He liked feeling that he belonged. Nine years of wandering the globe had been long enough.

Three days after the aerobics class, Cade was striding down the street at eight twenty-five in the morning. He was in a self-congratulatory mood. Last night was the first night he hadn't dreamed about Lori, one of the highly erotic dreams that had haunted his sleep ever since he'd bumped into her at the gym. The cure was working. The past was assuming its proper place. Today he'd ask Miguel about his sister.

He glanced down a side street to check on the progress of the chrysanthemums that for the last few days had been a glorious tangle of scarlet, yellow and bronze in the garden beyond a secondhand clothing store run by a well-known charity.

A woman in a blue jacket was crossing the sidewalk to enter the store. Cade nearly tripped over the curb.

It was Lori Cartwright. She opened the door and disappeared inside.

Lori? In a secondhand clothing store? Lori, who used to spend more on one dress than Cade's father earned in a week?

She must be volunteering there.

Of course. That was it.

That was nice of her, he thought, and found himself turning down the street. He was only going to take a closer look at the chrysanthemums; he'd like to start a garden once he was settled at French Bay.

He looked through the window of the store. Another woman was seated behind the counter, reading; Lori, still wearing her blue jacket, was going through a rack of girls' clothing.

He was watching a film that somehow had gone wrong, Cade thought crazily; its script had got muddled up with that of an entirely different film. A surreal film. Then, as if she felt the strength of his gaze, Lori glanced over her shoulder and saw him. The look of horror on her face should have been funny and was not. She ducked her head, turned her back and couldn't more clearly have told him to vanish from his sight. From her life. Forever.

Leave me alone...please.

Cade pushed open the door and marched over to her. "What's up, Lori?" he demanded with something less than diplomacy. "Ten years ago you wouldn't have been found within five blocks of a place like this."

She straightened to her full height, her blue eyes blazing. "How many times do I have to tell you I don't need you in my life? That doesn't seem like a very complicated message and I don't understand why you're not getting it."

"I just want you to tell me what's wrong!"

"The only thing wrong is that you won't leave me alone."

The woman at the counter said in a carrying voice, "Need a hand, Lori?"

"No thanks, Marta—he's leaving. Right now."

Cade grated, "The only reason I'm leaving is because I'll be late for work if I don't."

As an exit line it lacked a certain punch; but it was the best he could come up with. Cade strode out of the store and down the street, the chrysanthemums forgotten.

Had Ray lost all his money? After all, the recession was still on and bankruptcies were common. Why else would Lori be buying her children used clothing?

The reasons were nothing to do with him. Any more than she was. He crossed the main street, his jaw set.

Even though they'd been busy yelling at each other, he'd seen how tired she looked. Part of him wanted to sweep her up in his arms, carry her to his apartment and look after her, this woman who'd scorned and humiliated him. Look after her and make love to her, he thought with a twist of his mouth. Make love to her day and night, and to hell with her children and her husband. And if that wasn't an unrealistic and totally mad scheme, he didn't know what was.

All day Cade worked like a man demented; and he didn't speak to Miguel about his sister.

On Saturday morning Cade decided to drive across town to check out stereo equipment; he wanted speakers installed throughout the downstairs and part of the upstairs of the house at French Bay. After a series of the mild, sunny days so characteristic of September in Nova Scotia, rain was now pelting the windy streets, glistening on the tossing leaves of the maples and collecting in puddles because the drains couldn't carry it away fast enough. No day for umbrellas, Cade thought, and with a dizzying thud of his heart saw that the woman running toward the bus shelter was Lori, her head down against the rain.

I'm doing my level best to avoid you. To forget about you. So why the devil do I keep meeting up with you?

Because Halifax is a small city?

Because I'm meant to?

She was wearing her blue jacket and carrying a kit bag. She must be on her way to aerobics.

He glanced in his rearview mirror and pulled over to the curb, being careful not to splash her. Rolling the window down, he shouted, "Get in—I'll drive you!"

As Lori recognized him, shock fixed her features into a mask; rain was streaming down her cheeks as if she were weeping, and her jacket was plastered to her body. She turned her head to see if the bus was coming in a movement as jerky as a puppet's on a string. Only then did she grab the door handle and plunk herself down on the seat beside him.

Take it cool, Cade told himself, and said easily, "Just push that black button, it'll raise the window again. Do you get much of this kind of weather in Halifax?"

Lori fussed rather unnecessarily with her seat belt. "Not often," she said in a smothered voice.

She pushed back her hood. Her hair was a loose tumble of wheat-gold curls and her cheeks were pink from running. Every nerve Cade possessed tightened to an unbearable pitch. She was so close, yet so unutterably out of reach. Forcing himself to concentrate, he pulled back into the flow of traffic. "Are you going to the gym?"

She nodded, and again he was reminded of a marionette: this, in a woman normally so graceful. "If it's not out of your way," she said.

It was, and he couldn't have cared less. "You don't have the girls with you," he said at random.

"I was able to get a sitter." She shot him a quick glance. "Do you live near here?"

"On Whitman Street."

"Oh," she said faintly. "Where are you working?"

"At the garage on the corner near the Commons."

They'd pulled up at a set of lights. Without even knowing he was thinking it, Cade heard himself blurt, "Lori, if you ever need help for any reason, all you have to do is ask me."

The words replayed themselves in his head. He ran his fingers through his damp, untidy curls. "And what that was all about I don't have a clue. But—" he gave her a sudden, wide smile devoid of calculation "—I mean it. Every word. It can be for old times' sake, if you like."

She was staring at him, her jaw gaping, her eyes dazed. Hastily he added, "What's wrong?"

In a rush she whispered, "I'd forgotten your smile. There's something about it…it makes me feel…oh God, I don't even know what I'm talking about."

His heart was now racketing around his chest like a ping-pong ball gone berserk, and again the words came from a place far from conscious thought. "You can say whatever you like to me, Lori. I mean that, too."

She looked down at her hands, clasped in her lap. "No, I can't," she muttered, and to his horror he saw that the moisture gathered on her lashes wasn't rain now, but tears.

"Lori—" Someone in the next lane blasted a horn at him, and hurriedly Cade paid attention to his driving; the wipers swished over the windshield and the tires hissed on the wet pavement.

In a voice so low he had to strain to hear it, Lori said, "Forget this conversation, Cade, forget it ever happened. I'm tired, that's all. And I've always hated the wind."

"That's right," he said slowly, "you told me once how you got lost on a windy day when you were only little." The day she'd told him, he'd been polishing one of her father's cars and she'd come to get her little red sports car to go to a horse show. "You were wearing jodhpurs and a yellow shirt, and the wind grabbed your scarf—do you remember? I ran after it, and luckily it caught in the lilacs.''

''They'd been in bloom for over a week—it was a good year, they were like purple foam all along the driveway.'' She bit her lip. ''Do we ever forget anything?''

Another man might have missed the anguish underlying her question. Cade did not. ''Not much,'' he said. ''In my experience. But I would have thought your memories were happy ones.''

''Would you?'' she said sardonically. ''Then you'd be wrong.''

It wasn't an opportune moment for Cade to remember the night when he'd walked home alone through the woods; how the three men had loomed out of the darkness, taunting him as they'd backed him against a tree, laughing raucously as he'd gone down, helpless, beneath a hail of blows and kicks. He said in a clipped voice, ''We're nearly there. I hope your class goes well.''

Flinching at his change of tone, Lori visibly retreated from him. ''Thank you for the ride,'' she said with formal exactitude.

Then he was pulling up in front of the gym and she was climbing out of the car. He kept silent, his hands gripping the steering wheel as if it were a thoroughbred as volatile as the big bay mare she used to ride. Lori slammed the door and ran up the steps. Cade drove away.

So much for detachment. As for exorcism, he was going to exorcise that word from his vocabulary. What on earth had persuaded him to blurt out that ridiculous offer of help?

His eyes flicked down to the little finger on his left hand, the one that had healed crooked. Lori was the reason he'd been beaten up. She might have forgotten that. But he hadn't.

Nor ever would.

In a foul mood he drove to the music store, spent more money than he'd planned on the speakers, and took them out to French Bay. The wind had churned the sea into a froth of white and dirty gray; ragged clouds skudded across the sky, while the spruce trees that sheltered the house were madly waving their arms. The plumber hadn't turned up on Friday as promised, and the electrician had left a note that he'd run into a problem with the wiring. Wondering why he'd saddled himself with a rundown old house and ten acres of granite and scrub spruce, Cade paced through the empty rooms, trying to work out where he wanted the speakers to go.

He was having dinner with Sam that night, and with his mother and Wilbur tomorrow night. Right now he was exceedingly glad to be busy both nights. All the less time to think about Lori Cartwright.

Because the nights were unquestionably the worst.

That evening Sam took Cade to his favorite steakhouse. "Eat up, boy," he urged. "You look like you've been dragged through a knothole backward."

Cade raised his beer in salute and described the various problems of French Bay. Sam listened, offered some suggestions and tucked into nachos and salsa. They ordered second beers and the steaks arrived, along with steaming baked potatoes and crisp Greek salads. "I'm hungry," Cade said. "I didn't eat lunch, now that I think about it."

"You planning on moving out to the shore with a woman?" Sam asked, dumping a dollop of sour cream on his potato.

Cade's knife slipped. "No."

Sam said obliquely, "If a car's a real lemon, you sell it and take your losses. You don't keep pouring good money into it."

Cade had spent the latter part of the day trying to settle into reading, watching television or studying the stock market, all without success. "Consign it to the scrap heap?" he said ironically. "You speaking from experience?"

Sam grimaced. "Nope. After Bonnie died I never had the heart to get out there and start looking. Dating? At my age? Didn't seem proper, somehow."

Cade had the grace to look ashamed; he'd known what a blow it had been to Sam to lose his wife of many years. "My mother's got a new man friend," he said. "It's never too late, Sam."

"Miguel's sister's a real pretty gal. Hair as black as yours, loves to dance."

"And what," said Cade carefully, "if the car that's a lemon is the first car you ever owned, and you're not sure you can sell it? Then what do you do?"

"If you're a young fellow, you park it out back on blocks and get yourself a new one for driving down the street," Sam said. "At your age you don't want to be spending every weekend polishing the old one. Not like me."

It was on the tip of Cade's tongue to tell Sam the whole sorry story. But ever since he was a kid, he'd been in the habit of keeping his own counsel; he'd always done more fighting in the school yard than talking. "I only met Bonnie a couple of times," he said, "but I liked her. How did the two of you meet?"

As Sam began to talk, Cade listened; he was a better listener than a talker, he knew. It was one of his mother's complaints. Her other complaint was that he wasn't making any moves to present her with grandchildren.

Two little blond girls called Rachel and Liddy.

Sure thing, Cade. You planning on abducting another man's children? You know darn well when you go to

Juniper Hills tomorrow, you're not even going to mention Lori's name.

When Sunday evening came, it was a resolution Cade kept. He just wished it was as easy to stop thinking about her.

Another week passed. At French Bay the plumber finished the bathroom and the speakers were installed; at Sam's garage Cade made noticeable strides toward being accepted by the rest of the mechanics, a couple of whom had resented an outsider from Ontario coming in as Sam's partner. But Cade wasn't only a hard worker and highly skilled mechanic; he was also fair in his dealings, and knew when and how to put his foot down. After a standoff one morning between him and Joel, the unacknowledged leader of the other men, a standoff Cade won hands down, the hierarchy was established and even Joel started joking with him. Cade was pleased by this development. He liked the garage. Liked it a lot. The fact that it was a small gold mine was a bonus.

On Saturday he went in early to further his acquaintance with Sam's haphazard and highly original methods of bookkeeping. Cade had taken some business and accounting courses in Seattle; soon, and as tactfully as he knew how, he must suggest some changes. A computer, to start with. Revenue Canada wouldn't be amused by receipts stored in an old cardboard box that had once held engine oil.

At one o'clock he called it a day. He'd go to the weight room then go for a run; by the time he got to the gym Lori would have left.

He wasn't going to think about Lori.

But when Cade pushed open the gym door, the first thing he heard was Liddy's unmistakably shrill voice raised in outrage. She was sitting bolt upright in one of the padded chairs, her little cheeks scarlet. "He is so coming back!"

"He's not. Mum said he's not!"

Even Rachel looked upset; she was twirling a long strand of her hair with agitated movements. Then Liddy faltered, "He's my daddy. He can't stay away, not forever."

"They're divorced," Rachel retorted. "Mum told you all about that, you know she did."

Liddy looked on the verge of tears. "I don't care about their silly ol' divorce. I just want him to come home."

"Well, he's never going to," Rachel said sullenly.

At the same moment that Liddy burst into noisy and copious tears, Cade looked up. Lori was standing in the doorway that led from the front desk. Standing as if she were glued to the floor. Staring at him.

You lied to me, he thought, impaling her on his gaze. You're not a married woman, you're divorced. You're free.

Like two drums with different rhythms, the words banged at his skull. You lied. You're free. You lied. You're free. Dimly he wondered if he looked as stunned as he felt. By the way she was transfixed to the floor, he probably did.

Then Liddy saw her mother, too. She erupted from her chair and flung herself across the carpet into her mother's arms, sobbing, "Daddy's coming back someday, isn't he, Mum?"

"No," Lori said steadily, still staring at Cade, "he won't be coming back, darling. I told you that."

"I didn't think you meant it," Liddy wailed.

"I knew you meant it," Rachel said, slouching over to join them.

"He moved to Texas," Lori said with the same dead calm. "That's a long way away, Liddy."

"Cowboys live in Texas," Liddy snuffled.

"Your father lives in a city, darling. He doesn't like the country, remember?"

Rachel patted Liddy awkwardly on the shoulder. "We'll be late for the movie, Liddy, and you know how much you want to see it," she said and pulled a ragged bunch of tissues from the pocket of her jeans. "Here, you can have these."

Liddy scrubbed her cheeks with the tissues, Lori dragged her eyes away from Cade's and glanced up at the clock, and Rachel said in an agony of frustration, gesturing through the tall glass windows, "Oh no, there goes the bus—we've missed it! And we've waited all week to go to the movies."

She, too, looked about ready to burst into tears. Cade said stiffly, "I'll drive you. That way you'll get there in time."

"We can't do that," Lori protested. "We'll—"

Rachel gave Cade a dazzling smile. "You're Mum's friend, aren't you? The one who spoke to us the other day. Come on, Mum, you know how much Liddy wants to see all the dalmatians, and it might not be on next week. Let's go."

There were no flies on Rachel, thought Cade. "My car's out in the parking lot. What time does the movie start?"

"One forty-five," Lori muttered. "My class ran late."

"We can make it in lots of time," Cade said. His smile was mocking, because Lori was caught and she knew it. Once the three of them had been for a drive in his car, he'd be officially accepted as a friend of the family. As a friend of Lori, single mother and divorcée. A woman who was no longer the wife of Ray Cartwright.

Texas wasn't far enough away for the likes of Ray

Cartwright. But it sure beat Halifax. Cade felt quite extraordinarily happy.

Rachel grabbed her mother's hand while Liddy glowered at Cade. Liddy didn't like him, that much was clear. Cade knew very little about children, and in consequence tended to treat them as smaller size adults. He said calmly, "I know I'm not your dad, Liddy...all I'm doing is giving you a ride to the movies."

Liddy buried her face in her mother's jacket. "The movie will cheer you up," Lori said, "so we're going to accept Cade's kind offer...although weren't you just arriving, Cade?"

"Yep. But I've got all day."

"No heavy dates?" she flashed, then blushed scarlet as if she'd meant to think the words, not say them.

"Not unless you call dinner with my mother in return for fixing her car a heavy date," he said, and recklessly decided to call the emotion that crossed her face relief. "What about you?" he added.

"If we're going, we'd better go," she said crossly. "Blow your nose, Liddy." Liddy complied and Lori dropped the tissues into the nearest wastebasket. Cade led the way out to his car. He unlocked it, opened the back doors for the girls and showed them how the seat belts worked. By this time Lori was sitting in the front. She blurted, "Isn't this a Mercedes?"

How can you afford a Mercedes? That was what she meant. Smoothly he started the car and drove out of the parking lot. "I picked it up secondhand when I was here in June, and Sam, my business partner, worked on it in his spare time all summer."

Lorraine would have tossed her head haughtily without a hint of apology. Lori, however, looked ashamed of her artless question; the differences between Lorraine and Lori were beginning to intrigue Cade a great deal.

She said clumsily, "It was raining so hard the other day I didn't even notice the car."

"Plus you were surprised to see me." To say the least.

She said in resignation, "We only live two blocks north of Whitman, that's why we keep bumping into each other."

"Celtic Street," Rachel supplied. "In an apartment."

So his two sightings of Lori, once at the secondhand store and once at the bus stop, hadn't been coincidence at all, but merely the result of location. Nevertheless, questions were seething through Cade's mind. Ray must have left her well provided for; and if he hadn't, her father was a wealthy man. What was she doing living on Celtic, a street that was lined with apartment blocks? He'd checked a couple of them out before he'd found his own apartment, and hadn't liked them at all. Cramped rooms, old carpeting and cheap appliances.

She'd lied to him about Ray, and she was living in a manner that suggested she was flat broke. But she was single again. Free. He said, "You have no idea how delighted I am that your class was late this morning, Lori."

She said nothing, although her fingers tightened on the knee of her jeans. Ringless fingers because she was no longer married. He waited at the four-way stop sign, and turned left. A few minutes later he pulled up outside the shopping mall where the theaters were. "Have a good time," he said.

"Thank you," Rachel said composedly, giving him an approving smile. This was perhaps just as well; Liddy's look could have skewered him to the seat. Lori scrambled out of the car, clutching her kit bag. "Thank you, Cade," she muttered.

"We'll have that coffee one day next week," he said.

She shot him a fulminating look and slammed the door. He watched the three of them run up the steps, then decided he'd go right out to his mother's and start work on her car; he didn't feel like going back to the gym.

Divorced. Single. Free. Three of the most wonderful words in the vocabulary now that they applied to Lori Cartwright.

CHAPTER FOUR

CADE was whistling ebulliently as he drove away through the city traffic, and this mood lasted all of ten minutes. But as he surged up the ramp that led to the highway, two uncomfortable facts reared their heads. First of all, Lori had been free all along, ever since he'd first met her at the gym; but that hadn't caused her to encourage his attentions. In fact, she'd done the exact opposite. She'd discouraged him as actively as she could. And, secondly, for a man who was a loner he was getting much too excited about a woman who'd brought him nothing but grief, and who was undoubtedly one of the reasons he'd remained on his own the last ten years.

To hell with that, thought Cade. After all, he wasn't planning on marrying her.

What was he planning on? Getting her in his bed as soon as he decently could?

Yeah, he thought. Yeah...and remembered the intoxicating sensation of holding her in his arms that first day at the gym, and his own body's less than controlled and very instinctual response. An affair. That's all he wanted.

But he still had to plan a strategy that would get past her defences. Past whatever scars Ray Cartwright left as his legacy. And past, he concluded with a rueful grin, Liddy.

However, although Cade had roughed it around the world, been in any number of tight spots and discovered within himself resources he wouldn't have suspected, when it came to evolving a plan over the next few days that would make Lori go out with him—even if only for a coffee at the cafeteria—his intelligence seemed to desert him. Instead his hormones took over every time, suggesting a very forthright course of action: throw her across his shoulder after her noon-hour class, take her back to his apartment and make passionate love to her night and day for an entire week. After which he'd ask some of the questions that were plaguing him.

After which he'd go to jail, he thought derisively, waiting for a traffic light to change on Thursday morning. He was later than usual because he'd been to the bus station to pick up some parts. Children on their way to school were dashing across the crosswalks, as noisy and colorful as flocks of tropical birds. Screaming at each other to hurry, a group of five girls ran down the slope to the road, trying to beat the light. Then one of them tripped, slamming onto the concrete sidewalk with bruising force. Cade's heart skipped a beat; unless he was mistaken, it was Rachel.

The light changed. Cade drove across the intersection, parked his car and ran back. Surrounded by her friends, Rachel was trying to pick herself up; she looked pale and dazed, a purpling lump on her forehead, her bare knees bleeding. Cade said urgently, "Rachel, it's Cade. Is your mum home? If so, I'll take you home."

The little girl looked up. Her lip was trembling, and she was struggling against tears. "I think so," she said in a thin voice.

To her friends Cade said, "I know Rachel and her mother and I'll take her home. Would you tell the teacher what happened? She can call Rachel's mum if she has any questions." Then he stooped and gathered the little girl into his arms. She was lighter than he'd expected. As her head flopped against his chest trustingly, he felt something melt inside him, an emotion totally new to him. Had he ever held a child in his arms before like this? A child who trusted him?

Rachel whispered, "I feel sick."

Every scrap of color had drained from her face. He said gently, "You landed with a real thump, Rachel, no wonder you feel so bad. I'll get you home in no time."

With the same gentleness he put her in the front seat. Then he drove to Celtic Street. Tears were seeping down Rachel's cheeks; his heart twisted with compassion. "Which apartment?" he asked.

"The middle block. Number twenty-six. I want my m-mother."

"Two minutes," Cade said, and parked on the street. He carried Rachel up the steps, pushed the security button and waited for Lori's response. He was about to push the button a second time when her voice, garbled by the intercom, said, "Yes?"

"Lori, it's Cade. Rachel fell down on her way to school, I've got her with me."

Instantly the door release buzzed. He went through and up the tiled stairs, which needed washing. As he entered the hallway of the second floor, Lori was hurrying to meet them, her eyes widening with anxiety as she saw Cade carrying her daughter. "It's all right," he said, "nothing serious."

Her hair was a mass of wet tumbled curls and she was wearing a jade-green cotton robe belted around her waist. Breathlessly she said, "Thank heavens I heard you, I'd just got out of the shower. Rachel, sweetheart, what have you done to yourself?"

Rachel's tears overflowed; Cade took her into the apartment, where Lori hurriedly moved some papers and a very large cat from the sofa so he could put the little girl down. Carefully he did so. Moving back, he said, "Have you got a first-aid kit?"

"In the bathroom, third shelf down." Lori knelt to take off Rachel's shoes. "Your poor knees," she crooned. "And you bumped your head, too."

Cade had always possessed the ability to assess a situation quickly, a trait that had stood him in good stead more than once in his travels. As he crossed the living room he saw that the furniture was sparse and inexpensive. A desk with a computer and printer was jammed into one corner. The bathroom had a plastic shower curtain brightly patterned with parrots and macaws; but the towels were far from new. He found the first-aid kit and resisted the temptation to check out the two bedrooms. One of which must be Lori's.

In the kitchen he put on the kettle, then broke up ice cubes and put them in a plastic bag, covering it with a cloth. After he'd gone back into the living room he said, "Here, Rachel, lie back and put this on your forehead, it'll take the swelling down... I'll boil some water, Lori, and clean up her knees. I'd keep her covered if I were you, it looked to me like she had a minor case of shock right after she fell."

Lori scrambled to her feet. "I'll get an afghan out of my room."

Cade fought against the urge to reach out for her. Her robe had gaped open as she stood up; he'd seen a flash of thighs and a hint of the shadow between her breasts. At the open neckline of the robe her skin was creamy white against the jade fabric. He managed to smile at Rachel. "Your knees must hurt."

As Lori came back and tucked a soft knitted afghan around her daughter's shoulders and a blanket around her feet, the kettle shrilled. Cade went back into the kitchen, poured the boiled water into a bowl to cool and picked out what he'd need from the kit. Then he scrubbed his hands at the sink. From behind him Lori said, an odd note in her voice, "You seem to know exactly what you're doing."

He looked over at her. Her expression was enigmatic. "I did a paramedics course in Vancouver years ago," he said, "before I took off around the world. Thought it might come in handy. Want to bring the water in?"

Although he did his best not to hurt Rachel and although his big hands were both deft and gentle, it was inevitable that Cade cause her pain removing the tiny flecks of dirt from the ugly scrapes on her knees. She bore it so stoically that he felt a peculiar ache lodge itself in the vicinity of his heart. A very long ten minutes later he was taping gauze pads over a slathering of antibiotic ointment. "There," he said. "I'm sorry I had to hurt you, Rachel, you were very brave."

Rachel gave him a shaky smile laced with relief that the ordeal was over. "It's okay," she said generously, "you tried hard not to."

Lori tucked the blanket over Rachel's knees. "There, darling, maybe you should have a little sleep. Shall I get Marvin?"

"Yes, please," said Rachel, and snuggled into the afghan.

Marvin was the cat, an overweight brindled cat of surpassing ugliness; he settled himself at Rachel's feet, purring as loudly as a car engine in need of a tune-up. Cade said, "I'd better call Sam, he'll be wondering where I am."

"Oh," Lori said. "The phone's in my room. Down the hall on the left. Shall I put the coffee on?"

"Yes," he said evenly, "I'd like that."

Her bedroom was very small; he could only presume she'd given the larger room to the two girls. The bed was three-quarter size and the room's only dresser was painted white. There was a photograph of her parents on it, Morris Campbell looking smug and prosperous, Marion placatory and slightly anxious. They hadn't changed much, Cade thought, and sat down on the bed to use the phone on the tiny bedside table, also painted white. At least there wasn't a photo of Ray.

When Sam picked up the phone, Cade said, "Sorry I'm late, I got delayed. A—a friend of mine, her daughter fell and hurt herself, so I brought her home. I'll be there in half an hour."

"Not all lemons are yellow," Sam said. "Take your time, boy."

The mattress on Lori's bed was soft, and a trace of her scent lingered in the air. Cade pushed himself up and went back to the kitchen, noticing on his way that Marvin and Rachel both seemed to be asleep. Lori's hair had dried in a tangled cloud around her head; in his absence she'd dragged her gown more closely to her throat, a move that rather pleased him since he didn't think it denoted indifference. He said, "Rachel's a lovely girl, Lori."

"So I've done something right?" she flashed.

She wanted a fight, did she? All right, Cade thought, I'll be glad to oblige. Not giving an inch, he said, "Guess you must have."

"Thanks a lot," she said sarcastically, and put mugs on the small wooden table. He sat down, openly watching her as she added cream, sugar, spoons and a plate of homemade cookies. Her color was heightened, her movements jerky rather than graceful. She poured the coffee and sat down across from him; she was chewing on her lip. He took a cookie and waited.

She slopped the cream and spilled sugar on the table. Stirring her coffee as if there could be no more absorbing task in the world, she said choppily, "Well, now you know."

"Know what, Lori?"

Her nostrils flared. "Everything about me."

"Each time I see you, I realize I know less and less," Cade rejoined with careful accuracy.

"Come off it," she snorted. "You already know I'm divorced. Now you know that I'm broke, too."

"I'd pretty well figured that out before today. I'm not totally devoid of brains."

"I've never thought you were, and I had no intentions of ever letting you anywhere near this apartment."

His eyes narrowed inimically. "You'd rather I'd left Rachel lying there on the sidewalk?"

"Of course not!" She ran her fingers through her disordered curls. "Dammit, I'm doing this all wrong."

She looked so ruffled and cross that Cade found he was smiling in spite of himself. "Why don't you try again? How about, 'Thank you, Cade, for bringing Rachel home and fixing up her knees...' That would do for a start."

"Don't make fun of me! And you sure as heck marched right in here and took over the whole shebang. 'Where's the first-aid kit, I'll put the kettle on, I'll clean up her knees...' I'm her mother, I'm quite capable of looking after her."

"Lori, you're like a wildcat. What's the matter?"

Her eyes were glittering like turquoise opals. "Cade, if you're not stupid, you're not naive, either. First of all, I can't stand it when the male of the species tries to take over my life. It drives me bonkers. Second, you're the last person in the world I'd have wanted to see me like this." With one comprehensive gesture she managed to indicate the whole cramped, cheaply built apartment with its minimal furnishings.

"So you've come down in the world. So what? Plus I've got no intentions of taking over your life!"

"I've come down and you've gone up. That must give you enormous satisfaction," she said with a bitterness that shocked him into a matching honesty.

"All right, so I hated your guts for years," he exploded. "Hated you and resented you and felt like a helpless pawn in the hands of you and your father. But if there's one thing I've learned in the last couple of weeks, it's that I don't hate you now.''

Well, thought Cade, that's interesting. Nothing like hearing yourself run off at the mouth to find out what's going on.

She put her mug down hard on the table. ''Why have you stopped hating me?''

''You've changed,'' he said bluntly. ''For the better.''

There were patches of color in her cheeks and she was breathing hard. ''I was horrible to you ten years ago. I was snobbish, arrogant and narrow-minded, and I was instrumental in firing you from a job you no doubt needed—although that wouldn't have occurred to me at the time. There's nothing like having lots of money to take things for granted. Like where the next meal's coming from and the clothes on your back. I looked down my patrician little nose at those of you in the village who were caught up in such mundane concerns. *I* was above them.'' Sudden tears gleamed in her eyes, and furiously she scrubbed them away. ''I was a bitch, Cade. A morally superior, grade-A, class-one bitch.''

''Yes,'' he said mildly, ''you were.''

She gaped at him. ''Well,'' she said, and a sudden gleam of humor flickered across her face and was gone, ''you don't have to agree with me quite so readily.''

''You were also young and sheltered, the product of private schools and of parents with an excruciatingly narrow and snobbish outlook. It's not exactly helpful if your father's ruthless and controlling, and your mother a cipher.''

She tossed her curls. ''You sure say it like it is. Or was.''

He held her gaze. ''I've got no time for word games. They're a waste of time.''

With sudden strained urgency Lori said, ''Do you really think I've changed, Cade?''

"Oh yes," he said slowly, "you've changed. Would we have had this conversation ten years ago?"

Her smile was rueful. "Not likely."

"I don't think of you as Lorraine anymore. Lori suits you better. Lori isn't the same as Lorraine...and I'm not talking about where you live. It goes a lot deeper than that."

Again she looked on the verge of tears. "I'm really sorry for the way I behaved with you," she muttered. "For the way I was. I'm so ashamed of some of the things I did back then."

In that generic word "things" was she including the beating that he'd suffered at the hands—and boots—of her father's henchmen? One thing was certain. He wasn't going to ask. Something about that episode still had the power to make Cade's skin crawl, and he was aware of a profound reluctance to even mention it. Later, he thought, later; and almost could believe that there'd be a later. Because what Lori had just said was a watershed in whatever lay between the two of them; he felt as though he'd traveled around the world at least once without ever leaving the kitchen table. He said, "I've waited a long time to hear you say those words."

"Too long." She looked at him through her lashes. "Even if you were in Chile and Australia."

"And Thailand and Singapore and Turkey." His grin faded as he added quietly and with complete sincerity, "You know what? You're forgiven."

She gave him an unsteady smile that reminded him strongly of Rachel's. "You're being more than generous."

"It was brave of you to apologize."

"I should have done so sooner than this. But I was so determined to keep you away from the apartment that I wasn't going to do anything to encourage you." She got up, blew her nose and sat down again. "I'm really grateful you brought Rachel home. And you did look after her very well." Her smile was sly. "In an autocratic sort of way."

"When you trek around the world for eight or nine years, you get used to doing things your own way."

When she'd stood up, her robe had slipped again so that Cade could see the soft swell of her breast pushing against the jade cloth. She must be naked beneath it; he tried to drag his eyes away, his throat tight, his whole body suffused with primitive hunger. Had he ever felt this way with any other woman? As though he wouldn't rest until he had her in his bed, as though she was his mate, the lost part of his soul, his completion?

His soul? His completion? Was he going crazy? All he wanted to do was take Lori to bed. Sex, he thought. That's all. A very simple one-syllable word. It had been a long time since he'd been sexually involved with anyone. Too long, obviously.

Time he remedied that. He glanced up. Lori was staring at him, her jaw agape, her blue eyes appalled; to have so thoroughly unnerved her, he must have been slavering over her with all the subtlety of Genghis Khan. Angry with himself, he watched her clumsily push back her chair so that it scraped on the floor.

"Cade, you mustn't look at me like that, it's not on the cards that—"

The chair tipped backward. He leaped to his feet and lunged for it, bumping against Lori's arm. From the door a child's voice shrilled, "Don't you hit my mum! Don't you dare hit my mum!"

The chair crashed against the stove. There was a brief, dreadful silence. Lori's eyes had locked with Cade's, and in their depths he saw sick horror and a flood of memories that made her press her palms to her cheeks and look, briefly, much older than her twenty-nine years. Older. Careworn. Exhausted. Hopeless. The adjectives ripped through Cade's brain in quick succession. He said in a voice he wouldn't have recognized as his own, "So that's why you left Ray."

"It was one of the reasons," she whispered.

Feeling as though all his muscles had seized up on him, Cade turned to face Rachel. The little girl was gazing from one to the other of them, frantically twisting her hair around her fingers. Cade hunkered down so he was at her level and said with all the force of his personality and with the kind of raw honesty he only very rarely exposed, "Rachel, I'll only say this once, but I want you to know I mean every word. I will never, ever hit your mum. Do you understand that? Never."

"Okay," she mumbled.

Her mother said weakly, "I thought you were asleep, Rachel."

"Marvin dug his claws into my leg, so I woke up. I came to get a cookie."

Cade got to his feet and produced a smile that seemed to stretch the skin on his face. "Anyone who was as brave as you while I was bandaging your knees deserves three cookies," he said. "They're very good cookies. Lots of chocolate chips."

Visibly the child relaxed. No child should have to feel that sort of terror, thought Cade, or have to come to her mother's rescue against a full-grown man. With a cold, implacable fury he knew that if Ray Cartwright were to step into the room right now, Ray Cartwright would be dead meat. He turned to pick up the plate of cookies, and watched Lori flinch from the expression on his face. Swallowing hard, he battled down the heavy pounding of his heart and the rage that was vibrating along every nerve in his body. It was the kind of rage that demanded action. But there was nothing he could do. Absolutely nothing. The damage was done.

He passed Rachel the cookies. She took three, favoring him with an impudent grin. "Mum only ever lets me have two at a time."

"Shh," Cade said, "it'll be our secret."

Giggling, she hobbled back to the chesterfield. Cade took a cookie from the plate and began to chew it. The alternative was to throw the plate at the wall. Or slam his fist into the table.

Not what Lori needs. Or Rachel. Keep your fists in your pockets where they belong.

Very carefully he put the plate down. Lori was gripping the edge of the table as if it was all that was keeping her upright; her face was a frozen mask. With fierce compassion he saw that she was shivering. As he instinctively reached out for her, she shrank from him, her breath catching in her throat in a way that stabbed him to the heart. He rapped, "I'm not Ray!"

"My head knows that," she said tonelessly. "But my body says to run as fast and as far as I can."

It wasn't a reply calculated to make Cade feel any better. He raked his fingers through his hair, moving his shoulders restlessly in an effort to rid them of tension. "I've got to get back to work, Lori. Or it'll be Sam who'll be firing me, not your father. But I want you to do something for me. Will you?"

"It depends what it is."

For the second time in as many minutes, he focused all the strength of his considerable willpower on someone else. "Are you free on Saturday evening?" She nodded reluctantly. He went on, "Get a sitter—I'll pay if you can't afford it. I'll pick you up around eight, take you out for dinner."

"I don't date," she said coldly.

So she wasn't going out with anyone else, he thought with a thrill of possessive pleasure. "Fine," he said. "In that case you can come to my apartment and I'll cook. I'm a pretty good cook," he finished immodestly.

"That still sounds like a date to me."

"Lori," Cade said harshly, "you of all women should know that I can withstand your charms."

Between them, called up by his words, lay that scene in the woods behind her father's house so many years ago, when Lori had done her inexperienced but extraordinarily provocative best to seduce Cade; and Cade, after an initial, unforgettable and scorching surrender, had pushed her away. Right now, if her eyes had held knives they would have flayed the skin from his bones. She snapped, "But I've changed. Or so you keep saying."

He raised his brow. "You're ten years older, for starters."

"Cade...low blow!"

He loved the way humor so swiftly glinted across her features; part of her beauty, he decided thoughtfully, lay in the very vividness of her expressions and the rapidity with which they enlivened her face. "The battle between the sexes has never, in my opinion, been overly endowed with fairness," he said. "Saturday. Eight o'clock."

She said tautly, "Why do I have the feeling I've just been railroaded?"

"Because you have." He grinned at her. "I'll look forward to Saturday and I'll see myself out."

In the living room Rachel had drifted off to sleep again, her thin chest sprinkled with cookie crumbs; Marvin was snoring. Cade tiptoed across the ugly shag carpet, snagged the latch and closed the door behind him.

He had a date with Lori. Nor was it just for a coffee at the cafeteria. And all his instincts had been right to warn him about Ray Cartwright.

He drove to the garage, marched the boxes in the front door straight past Sam and stashed them against the wall. "Well," said Sam, "you developing a taste for lemons? Or has the lemon changed into an orange?" He put his head to one side. "One of them big Valencias. Lots of juice, and they taste like sunshine."

"Lay off, Sam."

Sam stroked his bushy mustache. "At least you look like you got some life in you, boy—that's what I'd call an improvement. By the way, the tax guys got on my tail this morning. I forgot my quarterly payment. Can you look after it?"

"Give me a month," Cade said dryly. "We're going shopping for a computer next week, Sam. I'm going to teach you how to use it, and you're not going to make any remarks about old dogs and new tricks. Auditors don't like finding receipts in among the spark plugs and the windshield wipers."

"No sense of humor, that's their problem," Sam said, and started to sing, very soulfully, "You are my sunshine..."

Cade headed for the stockroom, where not even the deplorable state of Sam's income tax records could quench the glow of anticipation he'd been feeling ever since Lori—however reluctantly—had agreed to have dinner with him.

CHAPTER FIVE

AT THREE minutes past eight on Saturday evening Cade drew up outside the brick apartment block on Celtic Street. Lori was waiting for him in the lobby, and ran out to his car. She got in and gave him a bright smile that didn't quite ring true. "It's a beautiful evening," she said, "I could have walked."

"Only if I was with you."

With crisp hauteur she said, "I refuse to allow the statistical probability of violence in the streets to completely circumscribe my movements."

"We could have our first argument of the evening now and get it over with, or we could save it until after the main course," Cade said, all his happiness at seeing her spilling over into his grin. "You look very beautiful, Lori."

"Did you practice that smile in the mirror?" she said suspiciously.

"What smile?"

"The one that makes me feel I'd follow you all the way to Chile. On my knees."

She was scowling at him. He laughed, the carefree laugh of a much younger man. "I worked on it the whole afternoon," he said. "Too bad—guess we'll have to order pizzas for supper."

Her face fell. "We will?"

He hadn't expected her to believe him. Chuckling, he said, "It's okay, narcissism didn't conquer greed—I did spend an hour or two in the kitchen."

"One hundred and one ways to prepare hamburger?"

"Don't tell me you're yet another woman who thinks men can't cook?"

"I'll answer that question at the end of the evening," she said. "Pizza and hamburger are two of our staples. Rachel adores chili and pizza is Liddy's favorite."

As he stopped for a red light, Cade let his gaze wander over Lori's face. Her hair curled to her shoulders and her cheeks were delicately flushed. "You haven't thanked me yet for saying you look beautiful."

"For an older woman."

Her lips were painted an iridescent pink, while skillfully applied mascara and eyeshadow made her eyes look mysterious and depthless. He winked at her. "Makeup can take ten years off a woman's age, so I'm told."

This time it was she who laughed. "You're incorrigible! Just when I thought it was a real compliment. I don't get that many, you know."

"Not even from that blond hulk Tory?"

"Tory's in love with a seventeen-year-old premed student. He treats me as a combination confidante and elderly auntie. I am, after all, nearly thirty."

Her tone of self-mockery delighted Cade; the ability to laugh at oneself was, in his opinion, all-important. The scent of her hair drifted to his nostrils, and he was suddenly aware of how happy he was, sitting in his car beside a woman he'd been convinced he hated.

He didn't hate her anymore.

"I hadn't heard you laugh yet," he said. Although he'd never forgotten her laughter; it had the same throatiness as her voice. If a laugh could be called sexy, then Lori's filled the bill.

After pulling into his driveway, Cade turned off the engine. The silence sounded very loud. Her laugh this time was nervous. "You know," she said, playing with the catch on her scuffed leather bag, "this feels really weird. Going out on a date, I mean. At least, I guess that's what this is.''

"It feels like one to me.''

"I haven't dated since I was nineteen. I'm not sure I'll know how to behave.''

"Lori,'' Cade said forcefully, "I'm not going to fall on you the minute you walk in the door of my apartment. You're safe with me, have you got that? Although I'm damn well not going to pretend that I don't want to fall on you.''

"I see,'' said Lori in a tone of voice that said she didn't see at all.

"Look at me.''

In the pearly light of dusk she glanced over at him warily. "Remember that bloody great horse you used to ride?'' he said. "It had a ridiculous name...Thistledown, that was it...it used to bolt if a leaf fell from a tree forty feet away. That's the way you look right now, as if you're about to bolt. Lori, I'm not Ray.''

"I have never once allied you with Ray,'' she said, clipping off her words and looking considerably less than friendly.

Completely at a loss, Cade pressed on. "I only want you to feel safe with me. Even if you're ten times more beautiful and desirable now than you were at nineteen, and even if I am a normal red-blooded male who's been celibate too long for his own good. Safe. Can't you understand that? Can't you trust me that much?''

She said spiritedly, "Normal? Who are you kidding? If you're just an average guy, heaven help us poor women. You are without doubt the sexiest man I've ever laid eyes on...and I've seen a few.''

In a thousand years Cade would never have anticipated that response. He said blankly, *"Me?"*

"Don't you ever look in a mirror?''

"Only to shave,'' he said meekly.

"Haven't you noticed how the women at the gym—aged seventeen to seventy—watch you?"

He shook his head. "In your aerobics class I was too busy trying not to trip over my own two feet."

"After that class I overheard a bunch of the students in the women's locker room talking about you. Wondering who you were and if you were available. Lusting after you, to put it in good, old-fashioned Anglo-Saxon English."

Cade, who tended toward inscrutability, felt color creep up his cheeks. "Are you having me on?"

"I am not!" She grimaced. "Although you know something? I can't believe I said that. About you being sexy. I bet the etiquette books don't recommend that kind of remark on your first date."

"So are you taking it back?"

"No. But I should have used a different word."

Despite his discomfort, Cade was rather enjoying this conversation. "Like what?"

She frowned in thought. "Compelling. Magnetic...remember how all those little iron filings used to scurry after the magnet in physics class?" She shot him a glance that was a confused mixture of amusement and panic. "I always talk too much when I'm nervous."

"You don't need to be nervous," he said forcibly.

The amusement fled. "Nervous? Who am I kidding? I'm scared out of my wits."

"Because it's me or because it's a date?" Cade asked, and braced himself for her answer.

"Do they have to be mutually exclusive?"

He looked at her in silence. Lori Cartwright, whose self-possession had been formidable at age nineteen, was now admitting that she was genuinely frightened to be out with him on a date. She was fiddling with the catch on her purse; her nails were painted a soft shell-pink that he found very attractive. He said slowly, "Maybe we should start all over again."

With a wayward gleam of laughter she said, "Actually, I'm awfully hungry. Maybe we should go in and order that pizza."

"Maybe we should," said Cade, and got out of the car.

So Lori thought he was sexy, compelling and magnetic. To hell with the etiquette books, he thought. He was extremely pleased to have that piece of information.

Even if he did frighten her.

He unlocked the door to his apartment and she preceded him up the narrow flight of stairs that opened into a small hallway. He took her coat, being careful not to touch her—for her protection or for his—and ushered her into the living room. Now it was he who was nervous, Cade decided wryly. "I'll start the fire and get you a drink. Make yourself at home."

He stooped to touch a match to the paper and kindling in the fireplace. "Would you like a cocktail or some wine, Lori?"

She was standing in the center of the room looking around her. The chesterfield was covered in soft blue velvet, the Indian silk carpet was patterned in rust and blue, and two paintings of the Australian outback made vibrant statements on the cream-painted walls. In patent surprise she blurted, "But it's a lovely room!" Then, as though she were hearing her own words replay themselves, she blushed with shame. "Oh God, why do I do everything wrong when I'm around you? I'm sorry, Cade, it's just that I wasn't expecting—and now I'm making it worse."

He said in an emotionless voice, "What were you expecting? Built-in bar, posters of motorcycles, and a television screen as big as the room?"

In a flash of movement she crossed the carpet and

gripped him by the sleeve of his Thai silk shirt. "I didn't mean to hurt you! Cade, I'm sorry." Still clasping his arm, a contact that coursed through his body like an electric current, she looked around again. The oak shelves were crowded with books, ornaments and stereo equipment, while an antique pine box served as a coffee table; on it, in a burnished copper pot, deep yellow chrysanthemums were blooming. Flames crackled around the kindling and birch logs in the fireplace. Slowly her eyes came back to his face. "I opened my mouth and put both feet in at once, didn't I? But you know, you're not being entirely fair. I honestly didn't have any preconceived notions of what your apartment would be like...that was one of the reasons I was scared, because I didn't know what to expect."

She was standing so close to him that Cade caught the herbal essence of her shampoo and, more dangerous, the fragrance of her skin, subtle and sweetly enticing. The firelight spangled her hair; tiny flames danced in her eyes. Desire hit him with the force of a mallet, stunning him with its single, powerful imperative. He was losing himself, he thought desperately, and with all his willpower concentrated on the whirling sparks in the chimney. On anything other than Lori. Because he'd told her she was safe with him, and could trust him.

Pulling back from her so quickly that her hand dropped to her side, he said hoarsely, "Can I get you a drink?"

She had never been a stupid woman. Comprehension widened her eyes, followed by a wash of fear that shocked him with its intensity. But then she took a slow, deliberate breath and with a courage he could only admire said gravely, "I think we both need a drink. White wine would be fine. And, Cade, can we start over again for the second time? I'd love you to tell me about all the treasures in this room."

Inarticulate with gratitude that she had accepted his desire for her without pretense or coyness, and without running away from it, he mumbled, "I'll be right back."

In the kitchen he took a platter of smoked salmon out of the refrigerator and poured two glasses of Chablis. When he carried them into the living room Lori was stationed by the bookshelves, turning over in her hands his most prized Inuit carving, a stylized ptarmigan fashioned from a walrus tusk. "I got that in Baffin Island," he said. "Even in the first year of my travels I was sure that sometime I'd come home. So as I found them, I'd ship things back to my mother. This apartment is the first time they've all been together...the year I spent in Toronto didn't really count."

She picked up a jade figure of the Buddha. "And this?"

Her interest was genuine. Gradually Cade began to talk about some of his experiences, from the rainforests of Thailand to the teeming slums of Calcutta. They had more wine and tucked into smoked salmon and squares of rye bread; he added another log to the fire, telling her about his first hilarious encounter with a llama and his love for the mountains of southern Chile. "It was in Chile that I first encountered Neruda's poetry," he said.

"I saw you had a couple of his books in Spanish," Lori said.

"Yeah...I learned enough Spanish to get by on."

"And all those books on the bottom shelf about accounting and music and wildlife? What about them?"

"I'm talking too much," he said abruptly.

"Cade," Lori said vigorously, picking up the last slice of salmon, "I'm having a grand time and answer the question."

Her throat moved as she swallowed. She was wearing a rose-pink shirt with an embroidered vest and a flared denim skirt, and she didn't look one bit scared of him.

"Well," he said, "whenever I could, I picked up university courses along the way. I was at a loose end in Sydney at Christmas, for instance, so I bought a ticket to *Messiah* at the opera house. That got me hooked on music. I studied accounting in Seattle, and the local wildlife interested me wherever I was."

She said thoughtfully, "You haven't gone up in the world as much as you're gone outward into it...no wonder you're changed so much, all the things you've done and places you've been."

"When I first saw that photo of you, I didn't think I'd changed at all." He smiled. "Regressed, if anything."

"Oh, you've changed. You used to have a chip on your shoulder as big as your father's garage when you were younger. That's gone. You give the impression of a man who's comfortable in his own skin, who knows who he is and likes it." She broke off. "Now I'm the one who's talking too much."

The unspoken message was that she'd been interested enough to observe and assess him at a level considerably beyond the superficial. Keep your head, Cade. She probably does that with everyone she meets.

Again Lori looked around the room with its eclectic mix of objects, all of them loved and all with a story. "I envy you your travels," she added wistfully.

"You must have traveled with Ray."

"Very little. I had the girls, you see."

Cade got up, picking up the empty platter so he wouldn't be tempted to touch her; her simple statement hinted both at loneliness and deprivation. "Why don't we move into the kitchen? I'm going to do a stir-fry."

She perched on a stool in the kitchen, which boasted an astonishing array of gadgets on the counter. "I always did like machines," Cade said, turning on the rice and taking the pre-chopped ingredients from the refrigerator. "Now it's your turn, Lori. How are your parents?"

"I haven't seen my father for over a year," she said rapidly, "and I only rarely see my mother. What kind of stir-fry?"

"Chicken." Not about to be deflected, Cade said, "Why don't you see them now?"

"Do we have to talk about it?"

He looked over his shoulder at her. He could see the line of her thigh under her skirt; her ankles were exquisite. He said, "I was almost sure you had to be estranged from them or you wouldn't be living where you are. Tell me, Lori—about them and about Ray."

"I'd forgotten about them for a little while—you made me forget them," she said with a violence that perturbed him as much as it pleased him.

He needed to know about them. But why? Cade wondered, rubbing oil into the wok. He wasn't in love with Lori anymore. Not like he'd been ten years ago. "Was Ray violent all through your marriage?" he asked.

"You go for the jugular, don't you? Unfaithful, yes. Violent, no. That only came at the end. Now that I look back I can see it was after he met Charlene—that's the woman he's married to now, her father could buy out my dad ten times over. Ray didn't want to be the one to leave, he wanted me to kick him out...so he turned mean."

"Bastard," Cade said, the stir-fry forgotten.

In a thin voice she went on, "Rachel saw him hit me. Twice. That's why she flew to my defense the other day. But Liddy never did, and I haven't told her. With the result that she still idolizes her father and doesn't understand why he's gone." She looked up, her face deeply troubled. "Did I do wrong, Cade, to keep it from her? She's so young, how could I tell her that her father was a bad man?"

Cade put down the bottle of oil and wiped his hands. Very deliberately he walked over to Lori, pulled her to her feet and put his arms around her. "You did the best you could."

"But I'm not sure it was good enough," she muttered, and with a sudden sigh of surrender leaned against him and closed her eyes.

She fitted his embrace perfectly; he rested his cheek in the tangled thickness of her hair, swamped by a host of different sensations: the tantalizing softness of her breasts against his chest, the press of her palms to his ribs, the supple line of her spine and long curve of waist and hip. His body stirred to life. This time, he thought, I'm not going to move away. Because I'm exactly where I want to be. I've come home.

Then, almost imperceptibly, he felt the tension gathering in her slender frame. "It's all right," he murmured, "I wouldn't hurt you for the world."

But her all too brief surrender was over. With a strength that surprised him Lori pushed him away, her pulse fluttering at the base of her throat. "You utterly confuse me," she babbled. "I have no idea where I am with you or what's going on. I don't *want* to need you or lean on you. I want to be free!"

And what could he say to that, he who'd roamed the world for nine years in search of freedom, and in the end had discovered that a hunger for the familiar and the known had become more powerful than freedom could ever be?

She plunked herself down on the stool. "The rice is going to boil over."

"Better the rice than me," said Cade, and grabbed a spoon.

"As for the rest, my father was furious with me for leaving Ray. In a way I've never quite understood, their business dealings were intermeshed, so Ray's departure cost my father a bundle of money. Dad cut me off when I refused to go back to Ray.'' She drained her wineglass. ''But my mother, for the first time in her life, is defying him. Not openly, mind you. But whenever she comes to Halifax she tries to see me and the girls, and she sometimes slips me a little money. Dad, believe it or not, still keeps her on a strict allowance.''

''Under the law, wouldn't you get half Ray's house?''

''That's the way it's supposed to work. But Ray had planned this well ahead. He'd remortgaged the house so drastically that I got very little for its sale, and then he moved to the States, where I can't afford to pursue him for support. I did auction the furniture, but I invested that money for Rachel's and Liddy's education. Or for the proverbial rainy day.''

''He did a number on you.''

Her smile was ironic. ''Didn't he? I'm not nearly the innocent I used to be.''

Cade's question came from nowhere. ''Do you hate him, Lori?''

She shook her head. ''Not anymore...I'm just grateful I don't have to live with him. I should have left him years ago, I suppose, but I kept thinking things would improve. And when all was said and done, he was the girls' father.''

Cade added the chicken to the hot oil. ''Would you like to light the candles on the table? And pour both of us more wine?''

Within ten minutes the food was ready, the chicken fragrant with ginger and spices and served over steaming rice. An alcove off the living room served as a dining area; Lori sat down and said appreciatively, ''You've gone to a lot of trouble, Cade, thank you so much.''

He raised his glass. ''To our first date.''

Fractionally she hesitated before lifting the glass to

her lips. Then she took a mouthful of chicken. "Delicious," she said. "Wins hands down over pizza."

They started talking about plays, movies and books; their discussion was animated, and Lori's frequent laughter delighted Cade. He'd made brownies for dessert, serving them with a thick chocolate sauce and ice cream. "I made extras for Rachel and Liddy," he said casually.

Lori's fork stopped halfway to her mouth, then clattered back on her plate. "You did? Darn it, why am I getting all choked up? I can't stand women who cry all over the place!"

Her eyes were swimming with tears. Once more at a loss, staying firmly in his chair, Cade said, "It's nothing, Lori—a couple of brownies, no big deal."

"It's not nothing," she sniffled. "I'm not used to being looked after, and all evening you've made me feel important and—and cherished, as though I matter."

He said levelly, "Was your marriage that much of a wasteland?"

"Oh yes. I knew on my way up the aisle that I was making a mistake. But I was so much under my father's thumb in those days, and—" She broke off whatever she'd been about to say. "I've got to go and wash my face."

She fled in the direction of the bathroom. Cade went into the kitchen and put the coffee on, then threw another couple of logs in the hearth. They finished dessert, making rather stilted small talk. "Let's have coffee by the fire," Cade said.

He hadn't yet found the kind of chairs he wanted for the living room; consequently he and Lori sat side by side on the chesterfield. As she passed him cream for his coffee, it suddenly hit him that the fabric on the chesterfield was the same blue as Lori's eyes. At the time he'd purchased it he'd simply gone for the color instinctively, knowing he loved it and had to have it.

This realization wasn't something he wanted to share with her. He said, "I haven't asked you about Rachel's knees."

"They're a lot better, thanks, she's going back to soccer practice on Tuesday... The fire's lovely, isn't it? The stone fireplace in the den at my parents' is the one thing I really miss from that house."

"When I move, I'll have a stone fireplace. Granite."

"*Move?*" Obviously dismayed by her tone of voice, Lori added, "You only just got here, that's all I'm trying to say."

"I've bought ten acres in French Bay. The house is being renovated, I won't be ready to move in until late November."

"Oh. Oh, that's not too far away. It's beautiful out there, isn't it? You were lucky to find a place, what's the house like? Is there a garden? Will you commute to the garage every day, do you think you'll mind that in the winter?"

"Lori," Cade said, "you're talking a blue streak. What are you nervous about this time?"

She glared at him. "You see altogether too much."

Only where you're concerned. "Confess," he said with a lazy and, he hoped, devastating grin.

She looked around the room, taking her time. Then she let her eyes wander over the man sitting beside her; Cade could feel her noticing every detail of his appearance, from his tailored whipcord trousers to his stylish silk shirt, open at the throat, the cuffs turned back at the wrists. "This feels so strange," she gulped. "You and me, here together like this. Every now and then it hits me."

Rather than strange, he'd have said intoxicating. "It's been a long time," he commented neutrally.

"I've had a wonderful evening." She drained her cup. "If this is what dating's like, I'll have to do it more often."

"Not with anyone else!"

Cade had spoken unthinkingly, from a volcanic possessiveness that she could so flippantly insinuate she might date other men; but he had no intention of retracting his words. Her chin tilted. She said coolly, "I have to go, Cade, I told the sitter I'd be home fairly early."

"I didn't ask you here just to loosen you up so you could start going out with other guys," Cade said in a hard voice.

"Oh?" she retorted. "What were you trying to loosen me up for?"

"This," he said, leaned over and kissed her full on the mouth. It was a move she plainly hadn't anticipated. For a moment her lips were frozen with surprise, before, insensibly, they softened in a yielding as tantalizing as it was short-lived. She then threw herself backward on the chesterfield and scrambled gracelessly to her feet. "You said I could trust you!"

"And *you* said you'd never ally me with Ray."

"If you behave like that, I will."

"It was a kiss, Lori. One kiss! Not the end of the world and for a moment you really liked it. I know you did. I could tell."

She opened her mouth, presumably to deny it, then closed it again. Cade said tightly, "I'll drive you home. How much will the sitter cost?"

"I'll pay for the sitter."

"If you're out with me, I'll pay."

Spacing her words, Lori said, "I will not allow you to take over my life."

Since when had a woman made him, in the course of one evening, run the gamut from compassion all the way to blind fury, with laughter, delight and desire thrown in for good measure? Never. And that was the truth. "I can afford it. You can't."

"I'm managing. All on my own for the first time in my life. Paying the bills, keeping a roof over our heads, and the girls clothed and fed. I teach aerobics, I work at the desk in the gym three mornings a week, and I do contract computer work. It all adds up, and we're getting by. It's extremely important to me that I keep my independence."

If he blew this argument, he might never see her again; it didn't take a genius in human relations to see that the issue of independence was of huge significance to Lori. Yet if she was intent on being independent, what place would she have for him in her life? "I'm sorry," Cade said stiffly. "I shouldn't have offered."

"But do you understand why not?" she said passionately. "When you were wandering around the world you were about as independent as you could be. I want the same. To know that I can do this on my own."

He had a knot in his gut. "Are you warning me off?"

"No! I don't think so...am I? I'm proud of what I'm doing, even though it's hard and sometimes I'm so tired I could cry. But I'm looking after myself and my children. All by myself."

He pounced. "Yet you said you felt cherished this evening because I was looking after you. Where does that fit?"

Her shoulders slumped. "I did, didn't I?" With a bitterness that stabbed him to the heart, she said, "I don't know that I've ever felt cherished by anyone. Except by the girls, of course."

"Lori," Cade said, "I want to see you again."

Her breath escaped from her lips in a small whoosh. "I can't imagine why," she said with the tiniest of smiles.

"Neither can I. But I do. Maybe we could go out to

French Bay next weekend, and I could show you the house.''

Her face lit up. "I'd like that."

"Good. Now I'll drive you home. And don't argue."

"No, Cade," she said demurely.

He put the screen in front of the fire and picked up his car keys. Ten minutes later he was home again. They'd said very little on the short journey, Lori had scuttled out of the car too quickly for him to kiss her again even if he'd planned to, and then he'd driven straight back to his apartment. But not even the mess in the kitchen could depress him. Because Lori had agreed to another date.

All he had to do was get through the week without her.

CHAPTER SIX

ON FRIDAY of what had felt like the longest week in Cade's life, he went to the gym in his lunch hour to do weights. By some judicious consulting of the clock, he managed to meet Lori in the hallway after her class. She was talking to Sally, the woman who owned the photography studio; she was wearing the neon-pink top again, the one calculated to raise his blood pressure several notches. As she lifted her towel to wipe the back of her neck, the line of her breast tautened. Cade slung his own towel over his shoulder and said, "Hi, Lori."

She pivoted; her smile of pleasure couldn't have been feigned. "Cade," she laughed, "why didn't you come to my class? Have you met Sally? Sally Radley, Cade MacInnis. Cade and I knew each other a long time ago, Sally, before I was married."

"So he told me," Sally said composedly. "The day he asked for a copy of your photo."

Lori's heat-flushed cheeks got a little pinker. Cade said, "Do you give your permission for me to have one, Lori?"

"To scare the crows away from French Bay?"

"It's a very good photo," Sally said. "I'll make a print for you, Mr. MacInnis, you can call in to pick it up. See you later, Lori."

Once she was out of earshot, Cade said, "She improves upon acquaintance. Would you like to go to the movies tonight? Four new ones have opened, we could take our pick."

"That would unquestionably be a date."

"A date with me," said Cade, "the kind I like," and flexed his not inconsiderable biceps.

"Rachel and Liddy are invited to a birthday party," she said rapidly. "It's at the pool, so they'd be out all evening. I have to work on an annual report this afternoon, so I'll probably be brain-dead."

"It's not your brains I'm interested in, baby."

"It had better be," she said sweetly. "Okay."

"I'll pick you up at six-thirty. That outfit should be banned. See you."

When he glanced back over his shoulder before entering the locker room, she was standing in the hallway staring after him, a bemused look on her face. Because she was so impressed by his manly physique? Or was she simply wondering why she'd agreed to another date with a man who challenged her independence?

They were late arriving at the theater because the mother who was to drive Lori's girls to the pool had also been late. Cade parked in one of the few available spots and they hurried toward the mall. Then suddenly he stopped, every nerve on the alert. From an alleyway between two buildings he heard a grunt and a bitten-off cry; swerving, he ran toward the alley. A group of at least six young men were punching a seventh, who was going down under a rain of blows. He said tersely to Lori, "Go call the police. Hurry," and headed into the alley.

He'd sensed, rather than seen, Lori take off like a deer. Taking advantage of surprise, he seized the nearest man by the back of his collar, punched him in the belly and watched him collapse in the dirt. Then, as one of the assailants whirled to face him, he saw the gleam of a weapon. His kick was both swift and instinctive; the knife flew out of the man's hand and Cade landed a hard and very satisfying right to his jaw.

But he'd run out of any element of surprise. Swearing

viciously, the biggest of the youths slammed a knuckle-duster straight at his cheek. Cade ducked. Someone's boot connected with his knee with brutal accuracy. Hurry up, Lori, he thought, and put into play all the dirty tricks he'd learned in his years of wandering around the world.

These might have been enough had he not been outnumbered. The victim of the attack had taken the opportunity to run for his life, leaving Cade to his fate at odds of four to one; Cade knew he was fighting a losing battle. He was damn well going to take as many of them down with him as he could, he thought, twisting free of a stranglehold and with all his strength swinging one of the men against the brick wall. Pain flashed down his arm. A knife, he realized, heard a karate-style yell and saw three more young men pouring into the alley.

For a split second he faltered. I'm done for, he thought, and felt something sharp rake his hairline.

But the newcomers raced toward his attackers, still yelling demonically, and with a crazy surge of laughter Cade saw Tory, the blond hulk from the gym, land a punch any pugilist would have been proud of. His victim, the biggest of Cade's attackers, the one with the knuckle-dusters, staggered; Cade finished him off by neatly tripping him so that his head thunked against the bricks. "Thanks, Tory," he gasped.

A wail of sirens split the air; swiping blood from his cheek, Cade saw something else: Lori running into the alley, wielding the flashlight from his car as if it were King Arthur's sword. Tory and his compatriots had the remaining two assailants nicely under control. But the youth Cade had first disabled had lurched to his feet and was heading right for Cade, murder in his eye. Lori raised the flashlight, a look of desperate resolve on her face, and aimed it in the vicinity of the youth's head; but at the last minute she screwed her eyes shut and hit him on the shoulder instead. As Cade snaked out a neat punch to the belly, the man collapsed with a sigh like a punctured tire.

"You'd better get out of here, Lori," Cade said, "before the police arrest you for possession of a dangerous weapon."

"You think this is funny?" she squawked. "Cade, you're covered in blood."

From behind them Tory said, "That's the last one. Too bad. You okay, Cade?"

"Yeah…" he panted. "Thanks, Tory, you got here just in time. Watch the guy with the black hair, he had a knife."

A blinding light blazed into the alley and three policemen with batons raised pushed Lori to one side. "Out of the way, miss. Freeze!"

Cade wasn't capable of doing much else. His chest was heaving, and blood was blinding him just as effectively as the light. His knee hurt. So did his arm. But he was also flying high on adrenaline. Leaning against the wall, he said to the nearest policeman, "They were beating up on someone, who didn't hang around long enough to say thank-you," and wondered if he was going to laugh his head off or pass out. One thing was sure. His jacket was ruined.

The next few minutes passed in a blur; then Cade found himself in the back seat of a police cruiser with Lori beside him and the scream of the siren lancing his brain. She was holding his hand. Not just holding it. Clutching it as if he might vanish were she to let go. Deciding he liked that sensation quite a lot, he mumbled, "Are we spending the night together in the clink? That's not the way I planned to seduce you."

Her fingers clenched involuntarily on his. "We're going to emergency," she said coldly. "You need stitching up."

More than his knee and his arm were hurting; he was hurting all over. He leaned his head back, which made him feel horribly dizzy. "When I was a kid, I always wanted to ride in a police car with all the lights flashing."

"You thought all that was fun, didn't you?"

Her voice had cracked; her face bore a mixture of emotions far too complicated to analyze. "Sure," he said. "Although it's just as well you got the police as fast as you did...thanks."

"Tory and his buddies were going to the movies, too. Like you, a fight took precedence. I *hate* violence!"

Cade said reasonably, "But you hit someone. With a flashlight."

"I don't know how I could have done that, I loathe people who solve problems by hitting out at someone else. People like Ray."

"You were coming to my rescue," Cade said, a touch smugly.

If anything Lori looked even more upset. "Does that condone it? The end justifies the means? I scarcely think so!"

Like a light bulb flashing as brightly as the red and blue swirls from the roof of the police car, Cade was visited by a sudden insight. Forgetting that he hated talking about that long-ago beating, he said, "You didn't have anything to do with those three men. Of course you didn't."

"Tory and his friends?" Lori said, puzzled.

"Remember ten years ago when you came to the gas station and I was in such bad shape? Two nights before, I'd been beaten up by three men who'd jumped me in the woods. Your father was warning me off, that's what they said. They also said you were the one who'd put your dad up to it. I believed them at the time. Especially after you came to the garage and—'' He broke off. ''What's the matter?''

She was deathly pale, her eyes appalled. ''My father paid three men to beat you up so you'd stay away from me?'' Cade nodded. ''But *I* threw myself at *you*—not the other way around!''

''Did you ever tell him that?''

''No,'' she whispered. ''No, I didn't. I was far too ashamed of myself.''

''So he concluded I was the one doing the chasing.''

''And all along you thought *I'd* had something to do with those three men?''

It was Cade's turn to look ashamed. ''I wasn't thinking very straight at the time.''

Distraught, she said in a rush, ''The night I tried to seduce you and you turned me down, I was crying my eyes out by the time I got home. I bumped into Dad in the hallway and said something about never wanting to see you again, and he kept on and on at me, like an inquisition, blowing the whole thing way out of proportion. It was awful. He was sure you'd forced yourself on me and I didn't bother correcting him, I was too angry with you and too hurt. The very next day he fired you. But, Cade, I swear I never knew about the three men, I'd never have done anything like that.''

She still looked horrified. As the police car turned into the driveway at the hospital, Cade said with all the strength he could muster, ''I believe you.''

''The day I came to the garage, I'd heard that my name was being bandied about the village and that you were fighting to defend me...*that's* what I was upset about.''

''Makes perfect sense,'' Cade said ruefully.

''But why didn't you tell me about this before?'' she demanded. ''You've had lots of chances the last three weeks.''

"I still hate talking about it," he said awkwardly. "Kind of humiliating for a young buck who prides himself on his fists to get his face pushed into the dirt."

Lori was still clutching his hand. She straightened out his fingers, stroking the one that had healed crooked. "I hate my father for doing that to you," she said fiercely.

In another of those blinding flashes Cade blurted, "Hate's the opposite of love, Lori," and heard the words echo in his brain. All those years he'd hated Lori, had he really been in love with her? And what about now?

His head throbbing like a diesel engine, he allowed the police officer to guide him into the emergency room.

Afterward, Cade remembered very little of the hospital other than the jab of needles that froze his cheek and his arm; and the wait on a cold metal table for X rays to his knee and ribs. The tear at his scalp line was stitched, and several more stitches drew together the slash in his arm. Nothing was broken or fractured, and once he was released Lori helped him into the back seat of a cab. The police, she'd told him, would drive his car home.

She'd stayed with him the whole time at the hospital, her face pale and set. She'd said very little. Through the pounding behind his forehead Cade now said, "What about the girls? You'd better get the driver to take you home first."

"We're both going to my apartment."

Discovering he felt remarkably like Rachel the day she fell down, Cade muttered, "I'm not up for being sociable...I need to be flat on my back in my own bed."

"I can't stay at your place and I'm not leaving you alone."

She sounded irritable rather than nurturing: Florence Nightingale on an off night. "I'll be fine on my own," he said as forcefully as he could. Although it wasn't a very impressive display.

"Cade," Lori said in a clipped voice, "I'm only going to say this once. You were extremely brave this evening, especially as it was all for the benefit of some jerk who didn't hang around long enough to show any gratitude. But right now you look like the lone survivor of a bust-up between two street gangs, and I wouldn't sleep a wink for worrying about you if I let you go home by yourself. So shut up and do what you're told. For a change."

His head seemed to be floating somewhere above the rest of him. "I'll never forget you swinging that flashlight. Now *that* was brave." Laughter quivering in his chest, he added, "It was quite a fight, wasn't it?"

"I'll never understand the male of the species!"

The hope that Lori might spend the remainder of the evening laying cool hands on his fevered brow was beginning to seem remote. Cade said fuzzily, "You don't have to understand us. You just have to love us."

Had he really said that? Or had he just thought it? Judging by the look on Lori's face, he'd said it. She'd be hitting *him* with the flashlight if he didn't learn to keep his mouth shut.

A few minutes later the cab drew up by Lori's apartment block. Cade fumbled for his wallet and said thickly, "I'll pay."

Her look should have withered him in his seat. "You will not." With crisp efficiency she paid the cabbie, got out and opened Cade's door, offering him her arm. He shoved himself upright, every muscle in his body protesting. "I feel godawful," he said, swaying on his feet.

"Really? You surprise me," she snapped. "Put your arm around my neck. Let's go."

They staggered toward the steps, which they navigated with something less than grace. A couple coming out the lobby were watching their progress; the man said something in a low voice to his companion, who laughed. Lori glared after them. "They probably think I'm bringing home the local drunk." Then she stopped in her tracks so suddenly that Cade banged his shoulder on the metal door frame. "Cade, I'm sorry—I wasn't even thinking about your father, I swear I wasn't. Why is it that when I'm with you I suffer from chronic foot-and-mouth disease?" She gave him a sympathetic grimace. "I suppose you must have had lots of people making fun of you when you helped him home."

Cade didn't want to talk about Dan MacInnis. Not to Lori. Telling her about that long-ago beating was more than enough for one night. "Let's go in," he said, "before I fall down."

"You're shutting me out," she said. "You might as well have slammed a door in my face. Don't you ever talk about him?"

"Lori," Cade said hoarsely, "if all you want to do is discuss my dad, I'll walk home. On my own. It might take a week, but I'll damn well do it."

"Okay, okay!" She got him into the lobby, unlocked the security door, then said in dismay, "The stairs...oh Cade, I'd forgotten the stairs."

"Not as many as at my place," he said. "Let's go."

The painkillers seemed to be wearing off; his knee hurt abominably, and in horror he realized that the sounds he was hearing were coming from him. "Sorry," he gasped.

"Only three more...there, we made it." She wiped the sweat from his brow with ice-cold fingers. "Remind me never to go to the movies with you again—I stay away from blood and guts even when it's fake. Just down the hall and then you can sit down."

When Lori unlocked the door, the girls weren't back yet; it wasn't quite nine-thirty. For some reason Cade had been sure it was at least midnight. Lori said, "I'm going to put you in my bed and I'll sleep on the couch. Don't even bother arguing.''

He managed a credible grin. ''You could share the bed and not have a worry in the world, the shape I'm in.''

''Huh,'' said Lori and ushered him down the hall.

''Bathroom first,'' he grunted.

As she closed the door behind him, he caught a glimpse of himself in the mirror. He looked like the ringleader of a gang rather than its sole survivor. Tough, beat-up and scruffy.

Trouble was, given the same scenario he'd lunge into the alley all over again with both fists flying; he'd never been able to abide bullying.

He was going to sleep in Lori's bed tonight.

Without her.

When he went back out, she was waiting for him. She'd turned down the covers on her bed and drawn the curtains; for the first time since he'd seen her charging down the alley, she looked uncertain of herself. As he kicked off his deck shoes then began unbuttoning his shirt, she backed out of the room. ''Leave your clothes by the bed,'' she faltered, ''I'll wash them for you.''

His beige cords and his shirt were blood-spattered, one sleeve ripped from shoulder to elbow. ''You don't need to do that.''

She said tartly, ''I'm beginning to think I'm a raw beginner when it comes to independence,'' and shut the door with a decisive click. Cade undressed to his briefs, left his clothes in a heap on the shag carpet and got into bed. He'd stay awake until she came back in.

However, sleep surged toward him in a great black wave, submerging him, and within moments his eyes had closed and his head had fallen to one side on the pillow.

*   *   *

Cade woke with a start in the night; Marvin the cat had jumped on the bed and was settling in the curve of his knees, kneading the covers and purring with uncouth vigor. A faint light chinked the bedroom door, which was ajar. From the pillow Cade caught the herbal scent of Lori's hair, and his body stirred to life. If she were here, she might not be as safe as he'd thought she'd be.

He was thirsty.

He got out of bed and headed for the bathroom. His muscles had seized up, making every step an act of will. In the mirror over the sink he looked worse now than he had earlier; his beard shadowed his jaw, and a livid bruise had surfaced over one eye. How to impress the woman in your life, he thought dryly.

Was she the woman in his life? With all the implications that phrase carried? *Was* hate the opposite of love?

Don't try and figure that one out at three a.m.

He took the three toothbrushes out of the plastic glass on the vanity, filled the glass with water and drank deeply. Then he staggered out into the hall. With a jar of his nerves he saw Lori standing there, wearing a white cotton nightgown that covered everything but her feet, her hands and her head; it was a far cry from her neon-pink aerobics outfit. "You wouldn't win any beauty contests in that rig," he said huskily, and reached out with one hand to stroke her hair back from her face.

Her tiny catch of breath sounded very loud. "I heard you get up," she said. "How are you feeling?"

"Just fine," Cade replied, dropped his hands to her shoulders and kissed her on the mouth.

She tasted sweet and felt sweeter. The touch of his lips rippled through her frame; when he raised his head, her eyes skidded up and down his body. She said, and he was almost sure it wasn't what she'd intended to say, "There's a big bruise on your ribs."

"Cade MacInnis in living Technicolor. Feature attraction at a theater near you."

"Very funny," she muttered. Then, to his utter delight and as though she couldn't help herself, she rested one palm on his chest, over the curled dark hair and the tautness of muscle and bone. Her eyes were like dark pits in her face; he had no idea what she was thinking. So quietly he could scarcely hear her, she said, "I can feel your heartbeat."

Even as Cade's pulse quickened, his body screamed at him to take her in his arms and kiss her as she'd never been kissed before. Don't be a fool, his brain screeched back. Can't you see the risk she's taking, the fear that's hovering just below the surface? Let her be. Let her learn to trust you. Don't scare her away just because your testosterone's hit an all-time high.

He forced himself to stand still, to keep his fingers loose on the delicate bones of her shoulders, and his breathing under control. Then she looked up. "Your body is beautiful," she whispered.

"Lori…"

His ferocious struggle for control must have shown. She snatched her hand back. "I'm not being fair, am I? I wasn't meaning to tease, Cade."

"I never thought you were…when you're with me I want you to do whatever pleases you. Don't hold back just because you're afraid."

"Is it that obvious?"

"Yeah." His voice roughened. "What was Ray like in bed?"

She stepped back so hastily that she almost tripped on the hem of her gown. "I don't want to talk about Ray!"

Cade couldn't bear the thought of another man harming her. Especially Ray Cartwright. Especially in bed. Yet why else was she as wary as a wild creature? "So we each have our secrets," he said.

"I shouldn't have come out here. But I couldn't sleep and I was worried about you."

Normally if a female started to worry about him, Cade ran a mile. But the fact that Lori was worrying about him warmed his heart. "You're quite a woman," he said. "You organized the police and Tory, you came in swinging your flashlight, and you didn't bat an eye when they sewed me up."

"Thistledown taught me to think quickly," she said.

Very gently he rubbed the slope of her shoulders, back and forth, as if she were as jittery as Thistledown. "On the other hand, when I make a couple of extra brownies for your daughters you start to cry."

"That's different!"

"If I were to kiss you again, what would you do then, Lori? Grab the flashlight? Cry? Or kiss me back?"

"I—I don't know."

"Why don't we find out?" he murmured, and sought her mouth. As if she were indeed a wild creature, he brushed the softness of her lips with hypnotic gentleness, his fingers playing with her hair. Then he let his mouth drift over her face, tracing its curves and hollows, its silken smoothness and its warmth. He kissed her closed lids, her tumbled curls and, once again, her mouth. His head was swimming; his very restraint enveloped him in a haze of sensuality.

Then like a jolt of electricity Cade felt her hands slide up his chest and link themselves behind his neck; his kiss deepened of its own accord, the pulse hammering at his throat and everything forgotten but his deep hunger for this woman, so long known, so much a stranger to him. Gathering her into his embrace, he roamed her waist's concavity, the swell of her hips, and with his tongue flicked at her lips, teasing them open.

With a sudden violence that entranced him Lori kissed him back, pressing her body into his. The warm weight of her breasts and her stranglehold around his neck inflamed Cade; he pulled her even closer, drawing her hips to his erection, feeling his control slipping. Almost indecipherably, wondering if he were being a fool, he muttered, "Lori, this is getting out of hand...is that what you want?"

She froze in his arms; to his enormous gratification he saw she looked dazed, her blue eyes blurred with desire. "What did you say?"

"I said you're irresistibly sexy and if we keep on kissing like this we'll be making love on the carpet."

"Making love," she repeated blankly.

"You and I. On the shag carpet."

She looked down. "It's the ugliest carpet I've ever seen."

"I agree. Do you want to make love with me, Lori?"

"Yes. No. I don't know!"

The tumult in Cade's body was subsiding; he discovered he didn't want to make love with Lori for the first time within earshot of her daughters and when his rib cage felt as though it had been used as a punching bag. Not on the carpet or in her bed.

He said carefully, searching for the precise truth, "I very much want to make love with you. But not here and not tonight."

"No," she said. "I suppose not."

Her face was unreadable; in her voluminous night gown she looked both virginal and unapproachable, her momentary surrender as if it had never been. Exhaustion washed over him, weighing all his limbs. "You'd better go back to the couch," he said grimly, "and I'll go back to bed."

Impetuously she cupped his face in her palms, her fingertips warm against the rasp of his beard. "Do you know how I feel when I'm with you? The same way I used to feel on Thistledown when we were cantering up to a jump that was higher than any I'd ever taken her over before…terrified and exhilarated all at the same time. The incredible freedom of soaring through the air. The fear that I'd fall off and break my neck." Her hands dropped to her sides. "I'm talking too much. Again."

"No, you're not. You always had courage, Lori."

"Courage or just plain craziness? Maybe Thistledown was my version of charging into an alley at odds of six to one."

"So we're alike…"

"Scarcely," she retorted. "I'm a divorcée with two kids, you're a loner who's never married."

"You're a rich man's daughter and I'm a poor man's son."

"I hardly think that's relevant."

Very pleased with her reply, Cade added, "At the risk of sounding banal, you're a woman and I'm a man."

"Now there you've got me," she said wryly. "I need to go back to bed, Cade. Liddy wakes up with the birds."

He rubbed at the tension in the back of his neck. "I won't be able to take you to French Bay tomorrow."

She hesitated. "Maybe next weekend?"

She wanted to see him again; that was what she was saying. "All right," he said and smiled at her. Her own smile was full of uncertainty. She turned and trailed back to the living room, and a moment later Cade heard the creak of springs as she settled herself on the chesterfield.

Supporting himself on the wall, he walked back to her bedroom. If he'd played his cards differently, Lori could have been here with him right now. But tomorrow morning would he have been able to look himself in the eye?

With a grunt of self-disgust Cade shoved Marvin to one side and climbed into bed. It took him a very long time to get back to sleep.

CHAPTER SEVEN

THE next time Cade woke, it was daylight. The door was ajar again, a small figure standing in the aperture. Liddy. "That's my mum's room," she said frostily.

Hoping that Lori had explained why he was in her mother's bed, Cade reared up on one elbow and said, "Hello, Liddy." She didn't reply. Stomping over to the bed, she gathered Marvin into her arms and marched out of the room.

Liddy didn't like him. Liddy wanted her father in her mother's bed. Not him, Cade.

His clothes were neatly folded on the chair. Cade got dressed, made the bed, went to the bathroom and then walked down the hall to the kitchen. Rachel said with gusto, "Wow, you look gross." Lori said, "Good morning, Cade," as nonchalantly as if he spent every night in her apartment. Liddy said nothing.

"We always have pancakes and bacon on Saturday mornings," Lori went on. "Coffee's in the pot."

Cade helped himself to coffee and sat down at the table. Rachel wanted to know every gory detail of what had happened the night before; Cade parried some of her questions, stressed Lori's quick-witted response and ate quite a lot of pancakes. But as soon as breakfast was over and the girls were cleaning up, he said to Lori, "I'm going to call a cab and get out of your hair."

She didn't argue with him; she, he knew, had noticed Liddy's antagonism and had tried more than once, unsuccessfully, to draw her daughter out of it. He said goodbye to both girls, kissed Lori lightly on the cheek and left.

Two things were very clear to him. He hadn't wanted to leave. And he was hurt by Liddy's attitude. Hurt that a five-year-old didn't like him. But Liddy wasn't just any five-year-old. Liddy was Lori's daughter.

On Monday morning when he turned up at work, Cade was subjected to a good deal of good-natured ribbing by the other mechanics. He grinned amiably, made remarks like, "You should see the other guy," and hid his battered face under the hood of a Porsche. Sam was late that morning. When Cade eventually went into the office, wiping his hands on a piece of rag, Sam looked up from the mess of paperwork on his desk and said baldly, "Good God, boy, what happened to you?"

Briefly Cade explained. Sam pushed back his chair. "You were a fool, you know that? Only a year ago someone got killed doing just what you did."

"Well, I wasn't," Cade said mildly.

"Don't you be so damn foolish again!"

"What's going on here? I'm not a kid you can order around."

"I'm still the boss."

Cade said succinctly, "We're partners in the garage and I'm my own boss outside of it."

Sam growled, "You're like a son to me, you stupid bastard—that's why I'm carrying on like this." As Cade's jaw dropped, Sam went on, "I watched you all those years, looking after the garage for your dad when he was off on one of his benders, covering for him, just as loyal as you could be. I used to wish I had a son like you...I wouldn't have screwed up like Dan MacInnis did. Hardest thing was to watch you leave, 'cause I knew it'd be a long time before you got Juniper Hills out of your system and came back to Nova Scotia."

Cade finally found his voice. He said gruffly,

"Thanks, Sam. I guess I always knew you were there, that I could count on you."

The two men embraced clumsily. Sam cleared his throat. "The income tax fellers are coming in a month's time. Think you can stop 'em from arresting me on the spot?"

Cade laughed. "I reckon," he said. "The computer's being delivered tomorrow, that'll help." It would also keep him busy; maybe that would stop him lusting after Lori and missing her, both with an intensity that scared him half to death.

As a direct result of all these emotions, Cade went downtown after work that day and picked up the photo of Lori and her daughters from Sally Radley's studio. Sally eyed his bruises with equanimity, framed the print while he waited and didn't ask for ID for his cheque. That evening Cade put the photo on the dresser in his bedroom; it belonged there, he knew. Although it didn't seem to help the hours pass any more quickly until the weekend.

On Sunday afternoon Cade picked Lori up to drive her to French Bay. Although she gave him a bright smile, and although her slim-fitting jeans and midnight-blue sweater suited her, she looked tired and hassled. "What's wrong?" he asked bluntly.

"You don't want to know."

"Give, Lori."

"Rachel's had the flu all week. She's just about better and she's bored out of her skull because she's read all her books at least twice over. Liddy and I had a fight because she didn't want me to go out with you. I was trying to tell her you were a very nice man when she burst out crying and slammed her bedroom door in my face. My computer went down this morning and I lost most of one file. Marvin threw up on the kitchen floor."

She heaved a long sigh. "Apart from that, life's hunky-dory."

"I'm sorry about Liddy," he said evenly.

"I should have told her about Ray when he left. Or earlier. Now it seems so much more difficult. She still keeps hoping for a letter from him...I wrote to him a month ago and asked him to get in touch with her, but he hasn't." She was playing with the seam in her jeans, her head downbent. "I won't stop seeing you because Liddy doesn't like you."

He'd needed to hear her say that. Through a great flood of relief he said, "But it's tearing you apart."

She nodded unhappily. "Sorry, Cade, you don't want to hear all my troubles."

All those years ago she'd been his fairy-tale princess, the girl he'd worshiped from afar. Now she was something much more complex, a woman of flesh and blood, with problems, faults and strengths; with a throaty laugh that delighted him; with, as she'd said, scars. He liked the woman much better than the princess, Cade thought slowly.

In a valiant attempt to throw off her mood Lori said, "You look a lot better."

The stitches in his forehead were hidden by his hair and the bruise over his eye had faded to a jaundiced yellow. He told her about the joshing he'd been subjected to, and then described Sam's idiosyncratic accounting practices, rewarded by her spurts of laughter. Before long they were deep in a discussion about computer programming, and in no time Cade was turning down the driveway to his house. He was nervous, he realized. He very much wanted Lori to like it here.

The narrow dirt track led through a grove of mixed trees, mostly spruce and birch, the slim trunks of the birch white against the dark needles of the evergreens. The birch leaves shimmered like tiny gold medallions, while the two ancient maples that flanked the last curve of the driveway were like scarlet flares against the October sky.

Then the track opened into a cleared field, part of a long-abandoned farm, with another grove of evergreens between the house and the sea, protecting it from the wind. Old lilac trees and the remnants of an apple orchard were, in turn, sheltered by the house. Apples still clung to the boughs. Behind it all, glittering in the sun, lay the sea, deep turquoise, edged with rocks and kelp and the lacy foam of the waves.

Cade had had the house reshingled in natural cedar, the trim painted white, and the chimney redone in beach granite. French doors opened onto a deck that overlooked the ocean. "Cade," Lori said breathlessly, "it's beautiful."

Her face was alight with pleasure, and something tight-held within him relaxed. As he stopped the car and they both got out, he inhaled a deep breath of the sea air. Lori said, "I thought from your description this was going to be just an old rundown place...it must have cost you a fortune."

"A fair bit."

"But—" Then she flushed. "I'm doing it again, aren't I?"

He said peaceably, because he had anticipated her response, "You want to know how a humble mechanic can afford ten acres on the ocean within minutes of the city. It's this way...when I was in the Yukon working in a tungsten mine, I happened to be in the right place at the right time and saved a little boy from drowning. His grandmother, a tough old bird who also happened to be a financial genius, took what savings I had and invested them for me. Over the years she's made me a lot of money that I never spent. Had no need to. But when I saw this place I knew it was what I wanted."

He grinned. "You'll have to meet her someday. She's a character, you'd like her."

Although he was keeping his arms firmly at his sides, his gaze met Lori's in open challenge. We have a future, you and I, that's what he was saying. Someday I'll take you to the Yukon.

Tilting her chin, Lori said, "You've traveled the world, you've worked in a tungsten mine, you've made a pile of money...is there anything you haven't done?"

"Made love to you," he said promptly.

Mischief danced in her eyes. "You had your chance ten years ago."

"And I blew it." His smile faded. "Or did I? I sure as hell had a lot of growing up to do, so maybe it's just as well we didn't get involved back then."

She bit her lip. "Are we getting involved now?"

"I don't know! I do know it was a very long week and I had a hard time keeping my mind on Sam's credits and debits."

"Or mine on jogging and knee lifts." Tossing her curls, she said, "Let's walk down to the shore. Then you can show me around the house."

"Your eyes are the same color as the sea," he said.

Color mounted Lori's cheeks. Very deliberately she stepped up to him, pulled his head down and kissed him full on the mouth. Then she stepped back. "I've been wanting to do that ever since you picked me up."

Cade said thickly, "You have this capacity for taking me by surprise."

"Good," she said sedately, "it would be very dull if you always knew what I was going to do next." Then she started down the slope toward the water, her hips swinging delectably in her jeans, the wind blowing her hair around her head. Cade, wanting to make love to her so badly he ached with it, followed her.

He showed her the rocky shoreline, the tiny sand

beach nestled in a cove, and the island connected to the cove by a jagged causeway of granite boulders. "The tide's too high for us to go out there right now," Cade said. "But at low tide it's a neat place to explore...as a kid I always wanted to own an island."

"Then I'm glad you own one now," Lori said. "I think when you were young you wanted a lot of things you didn't get."

He shifted uncomfortably. "There's an old-growth forest at the edge of the property—a couple of wonderful old pines. Let's take a look at them."

"You know what? One mention of your childhood and you act like Thistledown when she caught sight of water—get me out of here. On the gallop."

"I don't like talking about it!"

"That, dear Cade, is more than obvious...oh look, is that a hawk in the pine tree?"

His childhood was forgotten. They explored the grove of evergreens and wandered back to the house. As they approached it, Lori began suggesting ideas for the garden; she was so knowledgeable and enthusiastic that Cade, who'd always prided himself on how well he managed alone, had a vision of the two of them working side by side, planting ferns and trilliums in the shaded areas, roses on the south wall behind the house, vegetables in the open field. Two people working together, he sensed, might well accomplish more than two working separately. And have more fun.

He didn't tell Lori this.

They entered the house through the French doors, which opened into a sunroom with a glorious view of the sea. Talking slowly at first, then more and more enthusiastically, Cade showed her the oak woodwork in the kitchen, the ceramic tiles in the bathroom, the great granite fireplace in the living room and the smaller fireplace in the master bedroom, which also overlooked the ocean. There was a futon and bedding on the floor. He said, "Sometimes, despite the shavings and plaster dust, I sleep out here. You can hear the waves when the windows are open."

The sunlight lay in a brilliant square on the patchwork quilt. "Oh," said Lori nervously, and backed up without watching what she was doing. She tripped over the protruding end of a pile of planks and with a yelp of dismay started to fall. Cade grabbed for her. But her momentum carried her downward to the futon so that he fell on top of her, her body twisted beneath him. Laughing, he pinioned her arms over her head and bent to kiss her.

She lashed out with her knee and screamed.

Cade's whole body froze. The scream seemed to hang in the sunlit air; distantly, through it, he heard the rhythm of the waves. Then Lori began to cry, harsh, ugly sobs that tore at her throat, tears streaming down her cheeks. He shifted his weight and drew her against his chest, smoothing her hair, trying to comfort her as much by the tone of his voice as by his words, his heart cold within him. As, gradually, she quietened, he fished in his pockets and came up with some Kleenex. She blew her nose and scrubbed at her cheeks, avoiding his eyes.

He said flatly, "Did Ray rape you?"

She nodded, the smallest of movements. "Yes. Although he would have called it exercising his husbandly rights."

"But you wouldn't. And neither would I."

"We hadn't been sleeping together for months. But I still hadn't left him, you see, and he was impatient to be with Charlene. So I guess he thought he'd better turn the heat up. It was...awful. I left him the very next day. When you pinned my arms over my head...that reminded me."

Sick to his soul, Cade rolled away from her and sat

up. In a small voice Lori said, "Shouldn't I have told you? You always said I could tell you anything."

"How can I ever touch you again, now that I know what he did?"

Lori sat up, too, grabbing his sleeve so that he had to look at her; the tip of her nose was red and her eyes red-rimmed. "You're not Ray, Cade. You never were."

"You keep saying that. But it seems to me you keep confusing the two of us, too."

"I don't mean to," she said desperately. "You're the man who had the decency not to take advantage of me when I threw myself at you all those years ago. And got nothing but grief for it."

As he made a noncommittal noise in his throat, she added in an obvious effort to lower the level of emotion, "Tell me something...why did you hang around Juniper Hills after the beating? Why didn't you leave right then?"

"I didn't leave until after my dad died."

Swift comprehension dawned on her face. "Of course. You were the one who kept the garage going when he was drinking, I never thought of that."

"No reason why you should."

"You were very loyal," she said softly. "What was it like, all those years?"

"Lori, all I can think about right now is Ray."

What he wanted to do was pound his fists into the mattress, smash rocks with a pickax, run until he dropped. Anything to rid himself of the rage that had ripped through his body at the thought of what Ray Cartwright had done to Lori.

Action. He craved action. Not talk.

"Ray did a terrible thing. But it got me out of a lousy marriage, and since then I've come to terms with it."

"Sure—that's why you screamed your head off when I fell on top of you."

"You took me by surprise," she said in exasperation. "I should have told you sooner, but I didn't know how. It's not exactly dinner table conversation."

"It's the ultimate abuse of power!" Worse than bullies in the school grounds, worse than three hired thugs. Worse by far.

"I couldn't agree more. But you'd never do that to me, Cade, and now can we please talk about your father for a change?"

"No," he said.

Her nostrils flared, reminding him crazily of Thistledown. "So you want me to tell you all about my life, but you won't do the reverse? That's a great basis for involvement. Or whatever the heck we're doing here together."

Despite himself, some of his anger escaped. "I've always kept stuff to myself, ever since I was a kid," he exploded. "I can't change that."

"It's not that you can't. You won't," she flashed.

"All right. I won't. I bloody well don't want to!"

She scrambled to her feet; with one small part of his brain Cade didn't think he'd ever seen her look angrier. Or more magnificent. "Then let's not kid ourselves that we're involved," she stormed. "I've already had one relationship that was a one-way street. I don't need another."

Distantly aware that he was behaving reprehensibly, Cade said, "So I am like Ray."

"You twist everything I say!"

Is that what he was doing? Cade made a huge effort to calm down, forcing breath into his lungs, striving for rationality. "Talking about my dad won't make any of it go away."

"Of course it won't," she snapped. "It'll show that you trust me, though."

"You think I don't?" he said incredulously.

"If you don't tell me the bad stuff along with the good, you're only giving me half of you. You've got to tell me everything, Cade...it's called intimacy. Making yourself vulnerable to another person because you know she'll never use it against you."

"I buried all that stuff about my dad a long time ago," he said through gritted teeth.

"So disinter it," Lori said with a lightness that didn't quite ring true.

"I don't know why you're making such an all-fired big deal of this," he seethed, raking his fingers through his hair.

"Because it's basic," she cried. "You can't have involvement without intimacy. I've just told you the absolutely worst thing that's ever happened to me...I need you to do the same."

"I won't do that!"

"If you won't expose your needs and your secrets to me, or even admit you've got any, we're at a dead end. Can't you *see* that?"

"I know what I need," he grated. "To make love to you."

"Oh, that's just lovely," she said wildly. "Making love can be the loneliest occupation in the world if your partner's a stranger, if he won't share anything of himself but his body. Trust me. I know."

Cade thrust his hands into his pockets. How could he ever put into words the shame of his father's drunkenness, the dread of the bullying he'd suffered in the school yard, his desperate longing for normality, for a father he could depend on? "You're comparing me to Ray again," he said.

"Maybe I am..." Her shoulders slumped in defeat. "Let's end this, we aren't getting anywhere and I don't know how else to convince you how important it is to me." She looked straight at him, tension in every line of her body. "I don't want to see you anymore, not after today. Not if you won't change, or admit you're a hurting human being like the rest of us."

Frustrated beyond measure, not quite prepared to admit that he was also frightened beyond measure, Cade said, "Give us more time, Lori, for Pete's sake!"

"That's the one thing I can't do. Because I don't come on my own, Cade, I come with two daughters and I can't afford to experiment with men. Liddy's already upset and Rachel's getting too fond of you by far."

He didn't like being lumped with other men as some kind of experiment. "You're treating me like a pet poodle. If I behave myself, I get a biscuit...but if I don't, I'm exiled to the kennel."

She winced. "My father and Ray never shared themselves with me, not once. I won't put up with that again. Not for anyone."

She means it, Cade thought. This is it. It's over. In a voice he scarcely recognized as his own, he said, "Is this some kind of twisted revenge? I turned you down ten years ago and now it's your turn?"

She paled. "How can you even think such a thing?"

He hadn't thought. The words had just spilled from the aching hollow in his gut. "I—"

Frantically she interrupted him. "I can't take any more of this! I want to go home, Cade. Now!"

"Now can't be too soon," he snarled. "You women are all the same. Tell me this, tell me that, until a guy can't call his soul his own."

"You can damn well have the rest of your life to call your soul your own, and good luck to you," Lori raged. She took the stairs two at a time, stalked through the sunroom and shoved one of the French doors open.

Cade locked the doors behind him, got in the car and pivoted in the driveway, gravel spitting from his tires. He then drove home more moderately, although in a stony-eyed silence. When he stopped outside her apartment, she got out, said in a frigid voice, "It's been an education, Cade. Goodbye," and ran up the steps without a backward look.

Cade drove to the gym, got his gear from his locker and ran up and down every hill in the park until he was too tired to run another step. Too tired to think. Too tired to even pick up a rock, let alone smash it.

CHAPTER EIGHT

THE next three days Cade worked like a fiend at the garage, morning, afternoon and evening; and the whole time he refused to allow himself to feel anything but anger. Lori had taken a very minor issue and blown it way out of proportion. Ridiculously out of proportion. Whatever it was she wanted, he sure wasn't the man to give it to her; he was, in consequence, well rid of her. That he was sleeping badly, that he was being revisited by nightmares he hadn't had since he was a kid, and that life had lost all its savor, Cade somehow managed to ignore.

Through all this, he did make huge inroads on Sam's books. After one look at Cade's face on Monday morning, Sam's only comment had been, "Well, looks like lemons are back to being lemons. There's this book I heard about, something to do with men and Mars, maybe you should pick yourself up a copy."

"I have neither the time nor the interest," Cade had said in a staccato voice, turning on the computer.

However, early Wednesday evening Cade made a mistake in his programming, a stupid mistake he shouldn't have made, and realized he was too exhausted to fix it. He buried his head in his hands, hearing the silence of the garage echo around him. Lori, he thought. Oh God, Lori...

Pain swept through him, drowning him until he was nothing but pain. I've lost her...I was a damned fool. I handled it all wrong and I lost her.

How could I have handled it right?

You could have told her about the Martin brothers

waiting for you after school with all their cronies. You
could have told her how you never got to play hockey
with the other boys because you had to pump gas for
your dad. That would have been a start.

To have told her even those two small things would
have been breaking the habits of a lifetime. But hadn't
the last three days been breaking those habits, too? He'd
never in his life been in such awful shape as he was
now. Not even ten years ago, when Lorraine Campbell
had married Ray Cartwright, and every nerve in his body
had cried out that she was making a terrible mistake.

Restlessly Cade got up from the chair, trying to banish
the ache in the pit of his stomach by pacing up and down
Sam's office. He felt like a bear in a cage. Exercise,
that's what he needed. He glanced at his watch. It would
be safe to go to the gym now, Lori would be home with
Rachel and Liddy. And his stitches had been removed.

He'd been working out for fifteen minutes when Tory
came in the door. He saw Cade right away. "Hey
there," Tory said, giving Cade a companionable punch
on the shoulder. "You look better than you did that night
at the movies. That was quite the dust-up." He picked
up a set of barbells and for a few minutes the two men
worked side by side. Then Tory grunted, "Too bad
about Lori, isn't it?"

Cade froze with the bar at waist level. Feeling as
though his heart was being squeezed in a vise, he rapped,
"What do you mean?"

"Oh, didn't you know? She's had to miss all her
classes this week, likely won't be back before the weekend."

"For God's sake, *why?*"

Tory gaped at him. "Hey, man, you okay?"

"Tory," Cade grated, dropping the bar with a thud,
"just answer the question. What's the matter
with Lori?"

"Flu. That's all. No need to get all worked up." Tory heaved the bar to his shoulders, then slowly brought it down, his biceps bulging. "Thought you'd know she was sick—seeing as how you two are an item."

"Not anymore, we aren't."

"You oughta work on it. She's one neat lady."

Cade didn't want to talk about Lori. Not to Tory. Not to Sam. Not even to himself. He unbuckled the leather belt he was wearing, said with assumed calm, "That's enough for now, my ribs still aren't one hundred percent," and left the weight room. Twenty minutes later he parked outside Lori's apartment building and turned off the ignition.

It was only seven o'clock. Even if Lori were in bed, the girls would still be up. Although what in heck was he doing here?

In that split second after Tory had first spoken, Cade's imagination had presented him, graphically, with image after image of Lori abducted, raped or murdered. Or all three at once. The rage he'd been so carefully nursing all week had vanished, replaced by a stark terror that he was too late. That he'd never see her again.

Was he in love with her? Had he never stopped loving her?

If only he knew the answers to those questions, maybe he wouldn't be sitting here like a slab of concrete. Certainly when he saw her tonight, he needed to be calm and reasonable, the very opposite of the way he'd behaved at French Bay. Maybe he could run some errands for her, help her out, look after her. Protect her.

Arming himself with all these admirable resolves, because deep down Cade was afraid Lori might well refuse to see him, he strode into the lobby. Someone was just leaving. He slipped through the security door and ran up the stairs. When he knocked on Lori's door, standing in full view of the peephole, Rachel opened the door. She gave him a big smile, grabbed his sleeve and pulled him into the kitchen. "Marvin likes to run up and down the hall," she explained. "Mum's got the flu."

"I know, that's why I'm here…hello, Liddy."

Liddy gave him a dirty look, took a juice pack from the refrigerator and disappeared down the hall. She didn't exactly slam her bedroom door; but it was a close call. Rachel said apologetically, "She doesn't like you. She wants Dad back."

The kitchen looked like it had been hit by a cyclone; and Liddy wasn't, at the moment, Cade's main concern. "I'm going to say hello to your mother, then I'll help clean up." His heart pumping like a piston in his chest, he went down the hall. The door to Lori's room was open and the bedside light was on. She was asleep.

For a minute he stood there, watching her. Her hair was tangled and her cheeks pale. Her nightgown was considerably more revealing than the last one he'd seen her wearing; the ivory slope of her shoulders filled him with confusion, desire and panic. If a loner falls in love, he thought frantically, how does he stop being a loner?

As though he'd spoken out loud, Lori's eyes flew open. She said faintly, "I'm dreaming…"

"Nope," said Cade, his shoulders knotted with tension.

Shock, wonderment, joy, a panic comparable to his own: one by one they flitted across her face. "What are you doing here?" she gasped, and pushed herself up on the pillows.

He could see the dark circles of her nipples through the thin fabric; her breasts were almost spilling out of her gown. Swallowing, he said, "Tory told me you were sick. I've come to help out. If you'll let me. Please."

He'd never pleaded for anything from a woman before. One more habit bites the dust, thought Cade, and waited for her reply, wondering if his heart actually had stopped beating or if it only felt that way.

"We're managing fine," she said.

He couldn't bear it if she sent him away again. "Lori, I'm sorry I—"

But at the same moment she burst out, "Cade, did you—"

They both stopped. Lori gave a nervous laugh. Cade cleared his throat. His arms were rigid by his sides; he felt as though his whole life were hanging in the balance. "I'm sorry I was so angry on Sunday," he rasped. "I was a jerk."

Despite himself his eyes fell to the delectable fullness of her breasts; she dragged the sheets to her shoulders and said desperately, "Tell me the truth, Cade, please...did you miss me at all since Sunday?"

The truth, Cade. That's what she wants. Tell her how you feel—she's earned it. Searching for the right words, he said, "At first I was so angry with you I thought you'd done me a big favor by saying goodbye. But at six o'clock tonight it hit me—that I'd lost you, that I hurt all over worse than I've ever hurt before, that I didn't know how I was going to manage without you." He rubbed his forehead. "Miss you? Yeah, you could say I missed you."

In a small voice she said, "I missed you, too."

"You *did?*"

She was smiling, her eyes shining in the soft light. "Quite a lot," she admitted.

He sat down hard on the side of the bed. "Would you mind saying that again?"

She laughed, the throaty laugh that he loved so much. "You heard me the first time."

Like a man in a dream Cade leaned forward and kissed her, a lingering kiss that, among other things, reassured him that his heart definitely hadn't stopped beating. Against his mouth Lori muttered, "Cade, you mustn't, you'll catch the flu."

His smile, he was sure, stretched from ear to ear. "I've got a great immune system," he said. "Lori, I didn't think I'd ever see you again, and—"

From behind him Rachel piped, "We're out of milk and peanut butter, Mum. Breakfast crunchies, too."

He jumped, Lori blushed and Rachel gave them both a seraphic smile. "Why don't you make a list, Rachel?" Cade suggested. "I can go to the store for you. Do you need anything from the drugstore, Lori?"

"No. I'm over the worst...I'm just so tired I can hardly stand up."

"Don't go back to aerobics too soon, d'you hear me?"

"I don't get paid if I don't teach," she retorted with some of her normal fire. "And don't tell me what to do. You're not my father."

"Thank God for small mercies," Cade said. Raising one brow, he added, "Are you always crabby when you're sick?"

Flustered, Lori said to Rachel, who had been listening to this interchange with keen interest, "Please go and write down what we need, darling. Cade, my wallet's in my top drawer."

He opened the drawer, fumbled among her lacy underwear and found a leather billfold. She took out two twenty-dollar bills and passed them to him. Knowing better than to argue, Cade said, "I'll clean the kitchen when I get back."

"I can do that tomorrow."

"You haven't seen it," he said. "I'll be back as soon as I can." As casually as if he were her husband leaving on an errand, he bent to kiss her again; although for a few moments it turned into something that wasn't casual at all. "Keep that up," he growled, "and you'll have company in bed, Lori Cartwright."

"Don't forget the breakfast crunchies," she replied, mischief lifting the tiredness from her face.

In the kitchen Cade helped Rachel go through the contents of the cupboards and refrigerator. Then he went to the nearest mall. When he got back it took two trips to unload the car. Lori has to do this on her own, he thought, lugging the second lot of groceries up the stairs. Liddy sidled into the kitchen while he and Rachel were unpacking the bags; with Lori's money he'd bought everything on the list, while with his own he'd added several extras, treats as well as staples.

"Your favorite cookies, Liddy," Rachel cried; Liddy eyed them longingly.

He said gently, "Liddy, why don't you have a couple before bed, with a glass of milk? I don't think your mum would mind."

"I'll get you a plate," Rachel said.

Carrying the plate and glass, Liddy edged past Cade. "Good night, Liddy," he said. "Sweet dreams."

She looked down at the cookies, up at him, mumbled, "Thank you," and scurried down the hall. Feeling as if he'd just won the lottery, Cade arranged the bouquet he'd bought in a vase and picked up another small package. "I'll be right back, Rachel."

While he was gone Lori had brushed her hair, put on some pink lipstick, and covered her nightgown with a knit shawl. He put the flowers on the dresser and passed her the package. "I hope you like it," he said.

For a moment he thought she wasn't going to take it. "You shouldn't buy me presents," she said with a gaucheness rare to her, eyeing the package as if it might bite.

"Who else am I going to buy them for? Sam?"

"You scare me witless, do you know that?"

To his horror he saw a tear glimmer on her lashes. "I meant to cheer you up, Lori, not make you cry."

"I'm not crying," she said, daring him to comment as two tears dripped from her lashes to her cheeks. "It's when you're so nice to me that I get scared, I'm not used to it, and maybe I'll get used to it and then what? The flowers are absolutely gorgeous, I've always adored lilies and snapdragons and—"

"And you're talking too much," Cade said with a crooked smile. "There's no need to be nervous."

"With you standing by my bed?" She gave a breathless laugh. "You're enough to make any woman nervous. I don't know the definition of bedroom eyes, but you've got them."

"Good thing your kids are just down the hall."

"I love my daughters dearly, but if they were nowhere in the vicinity we might discover a new cure for the flu," Lori announced, took the package from him and started to open it.

He loved it when she flirted with him, adored the seductive curve of her mouth; but how was he to make love with a woman whose last experience in bed had been with a man who'd forced himself upon her? Although she claimed to have put that behind her, Cade wasn't so sure that she had. Any inadvertent move on his part might remind her of Ray; it would be like having a third person in the bedroom with them, a prospect he thoroughly disliked.

Inside the elegant green box was a tiny flacon of perfume. "Oh Cade," Lori said, as excited as a child at Christmas, "that's my favorite kind, how did you know?"

"I didn't. My lucky night—the cookies I got were Liddy's favorites."

"But it's horribly expensive, that's why I don't buy it anymore." Her smile was wicked. "Flowers and perfume...how very conventional of you. What are you up to, Cade MacInnis?"

How could he answer that when he didn't have a clue? "Scrubbing your kitchen sink," he said, winked at her and left.

Rachel had been putting away the groceries, gawking at some of his more esoteric choices. Cade looked around the kitchen, discovered the only dishwasher was himself and rolled up his sleeves. Rachel started telling him about her soccer coach and their last game; he asked several questions and was pleased when she picked up a towel and started drying the mound of plates and mugs. They were nearly finished when Lori appeared in the doorway, wrapped in her jade green robe. "It's past your bedtime, Rachel," she said. "Off you go, sweetie."

"Can't I finish?" Rachel wailed. "I was telling Cade all about Miss Pursley at school."

"It's late, darling," Lori said firmly. "Say good-night and I'll come and tuck you in."

"Night, Cade," Rachel said, "thanks for all the neat stuff." Impulsively she threw her thin little arms around his waist and hugged him; then she and Lori left the room.

Cade gazed after them. He'd liked Rachel hugging him; liked it a lot. He only wished Liddy would do the same. He'd never had much to do with children in his years of gallivanting around the world. Stepfather, he thought, trying the word out on his tongue. Stepfather...

By the time Lori came back to the kitchen, he'd wiped the stove and the table. "I'll come in early tomorrow and get the girls off to school," he said. "And I'll bring something in for supper after work."

Lori sat down at the table, resting her chin on her hands. "Are you asking me or telling me?"

In his mind Cade reviewed what he'd just said. "Well, it sort of sounds like I'm telling you."

"Sort of," she said agreeably.

"But it's all for your own good."

"You can scrap that line."

He sat down across from her. "Why do I have the feeling I've got a lot to learn?"

Suddenly serious, Lori said, "We both do, me just as much as you. But do you see what I mean about the girls, Cade? Rachel only hugs people she thinks are really special, and Liddy's got a major sulk on as far as you're concerned."

"She spoke two whole words to me this evening," he said dryly. "I'd call that progress."

With the fierceness that he loved in her, Lori said, "I can't afford to play around, that's what I'm trying to say." She grimaced, absentmindedly rearranging the salt and pepper shakers in the middle of the table. "I shouldn't even have started this, my energy level's zilch and I'm sure I'll louse it up. But having started, I guess I'd better keep going. I know there aren't any guarantees when two people get together…but if you're just playing games with me, Cade, now's the time to pull out. Before Rachel and Liddy get hurt."

She'd always been one to throw down the gauntlet. Hadn't she shown something of the same recklessness that night all those years ago when she'd done her best to seduce him? From the start that evening she'd made her intentions perfectly clear: nothing underhand, no subterfuge. It wasn't in her nature to be devious. "You know what?" Cade said. "I really like the way you operate."

"Going around with both feet in my mouth?"

"Being honest and straightforward. And very brave."

"My mother wouldn't agree. She'd be horrified to hear me asking a man what his intentions are. Nice girls don't behave that way." A smile quirked her mouth. "You note I'm not asking you if your intentions are honorable. Merely if they're…serious, I guess is the best way to describe it.''

He said flatly, ''I don't know what you mean to me, Lori, if that's what you're asking. I don't think I'm in love with you…although there's a real sense of connection. Of something that draws me to you and holds me there. And it's not just sex.'' He stared down at his knuckles where they were gripping the edge of the table. ''I don't mean that the way it sounds. Just sex. Some nights I can't sleep for wanting you.''

He couldn't think of anything else to say. There was a nick in the table; he dug at it with his fingernail. You're sure the last of the romantics, MacInnis. Connection. Sex. All the flowery words that women go for.

''I knew I could count on you to be honest.''

He glanced up; there'd been a note in her voice that made him suddenly uneasy. Lori was gazing down at the table, her eyes hidden by her lashes; she looked so touchingly vulnerable and yet so beautiful that it was as much as he could do to stay in his chair. Deciding to go for broke, he added, ''In all the years I was away, I never came close to asking anyone to marry me…in fact, I got on the first plane if I thought I was in danger of being seen as a potential husband. I never told a woman I loved her, and I never lived with anyone. I want you to know that.''

''I was never unfaithful to Ray. And you're the only man I've dated since I left him.''

''Well,'' said Cade, ''that kind of cleared the air.''

''Didn't it just?''

''But there's one thing we've left out,'' he said. ''Something very important. Basic, actually. What are your intentions, Lori? Toward me?''

She looked visibly disconcerted. ''I—I guess that is kind of a logical question,'' she faltered.

Quite suddenly Cade found he was enjoying himself. Matching wits with a woman like Lori could get addictive, he thought, and said with a gleam in his eye, "I don't have two children, I can assure you of that. But even so, I wouldn't want you to be trifling with my affections."

"Have you been reading Jane Austen?"

"No. Answer the question."

"But I'm awfully tired," she said, giving him a heart-rending look through her lashes. "I think I'd better go back to bed."

"If you're that tired, I'll carry you. But not before you answer me."

She said rapidly, "I am definitely not trifling with your affections and even to think of you in my bed makes me weak at the knees, not to mention the rest of my anatomy. But we're really only starting to get to know each other, Cade, and I haven't changed my mind on the subject of intimacy. Even if I did phrase it rather too forcefully the other day, I still believe it's essential."

"I see," said Cade. And he did. She was throwing down the gauntlet again; warning him that she intended to make him talk about his childhood. About his feelings.

She was staring down at the table again. In an uprush of tenderness Cade saw the hollows under her cheekbones, and the way the light caught in her hair. Connection was beginning to seem far too paltry a word for whatever it was that bound him to this woman. He said huskily, "Let me carry you to bed, Lori. Then I'll get out of here so you can get some sleep."

"Okay," she said, still not looking at him. "If you could bring supper tomorrow, that'd be lovely. The girls can get themselves ready in the morning."

Cade got up, walked around the table and eased his arms around her. With an exaggerated grunt he lifted her into the air. As she slipped her arms around his neck, her face only inches from his, he said, "You smell nice."

"*Very* expensive perfume."

He elbowed the door open and walked to her room. But before he put her down Cade kissed her, a long, slow kiss of mutual exploration. And, he thought dimly through a haze of desire, of commitment, commitment to another kind of exploration that wasn't necessarily sexual at all. Scared, exhilarated and aroused, he stooped to lower Lori to the bed. "Sleep well," he said. "I'll see you tomorrow."

"Thanks for everything," she whispered.

He let himself out and ran down the steps outside her building. There was a sliver of moon rising over the opposite building, and the bronzed leaves on the maples that lined the street were rustling their secrets to the breeze. From sheer happiness he wanted to stand there and serenade the moon. He'd been given a second chance. With a woman whose very essence had invaded his veins.

And he'd see her again tomorrow.

CHAPTER NINE

IN THE next week Lori recovered from the flu, she and Cade went to the movies and actually got to see the movie, and they went to a chamber concert at the art gallery. Cade cooked several meals in Lori's apartment, and took all three of them out for ribs and chicken at a nearby restaurant.

He should have been deliriously happy.

He was happy, right enough. But two obstacles intruded between him and perfect happiness; their names were Ray and Liddy.

Ray was in Texas, of course. Nowhere near Halifax. Cade was beginning to think it might be easier if Lori's ex-husband lived down the street; at least then he'd be fighting a man of flesh and blood. Any time he thought of making love to Lori—which was an almost constant and desperate craving—Ray got in the way. How could he, Cade, pull her against his hips, lie on top of her, enter her, without reminding her of how Ray had violated her?

Lori was physically fit and not afraid of asserting herself. But Cade was several inches taller than she, many pounds heavier, and she herself had called him tough. Besides, a harmless bit of horseplay at French Bay had made her scream in a way he never wanted to hear her scream again.

So he found himself maintaining a certain distance between the two of them, avoiding situations where he could have kissed her or caressed her; simultaneously it half killed him to keep his hunger for her so tightly reined. He knew he wasn't behaving naturally, the way he wanted to behave. Even so, he found it impossible to tell Lori what was going on inside him. How could he? He'd sound like a fool. Men weren't supposed to be afraid of making love...particularly compelling and magnetic men.

What he hated most of all was that he was allowing himself to be defeated by Ray, just as he had been ten years ago on Lori's wedding day. Such repetition filled Cade with impotent fury, and further tarnished his happiness.

Lori had never again asked him about his father; it was as though she were biding her time, waiting for him to make the first move. Cade was aware of her silence, and of his own even more so. Aware that there was a brake on his tongue. A brake that had seized up, he thought without much humor. He was a mechanic. He should be able to fix it. But somehow he couldn't.

And then there was Liddy. Liddy was a small, inarticulate bundle of resistance to Cade's presence in her mother's life. If forced to do so, she spoke to Cade, minimally and grudgingly; she never volunteered anything, and she escaped to her room as often as she could when Cade was in her mother's apartment. All this Cade was finding increasingly hurtful. So, he was almost sure, was Lori.

On a Thursday evening when Lori was in the shower and Cade had made hot drinks for the girls, he overheard Rachel and Liddy arguing in their bedroom. "You say thank-you when he brings the hot chocolate," Rachel said officiously.

"Why should I?" Liddy sulked.

"*I* hope he marries Mum."

"He can't!"

"I don't see why not. All he has to do is ask her."

"Mum's already married. To Dad."

Rachel sounded exasperated. "Liddy, they're divorced. That means they're not married anymore. I've told you that over and over again.''

Cade gave a couple of loud coughs and carried in the hot chocolate, trying not to notice Liddy's drooping mouth. He said on impulse, ''Liddy, let me tell you something. Love doesn't have to be rationed out—not like your mum rations the number of marshmallows you're allowed in your hot chocolate. You love your dad, of course you do. But you love your mum and Rachel and Marvin, as well, and there's always room for one more. Dozens more.'' He added with a smile, ''The marshmallows will just keep right on melting into the hot chocolate.''

Liddy buried her stubborn little face in her mug, emerging with a white mustache and a pout. If Cade as a boy hadn't suffered from a father who was never there when he'd needed him, he would have found it more difficult to be sympathetic. But Liddy pulled at his heartstrings. Refusing to allow her silence to defeat him, he said, ''It's great when the marshmallows go all goopy like that, isn't it?''

''Go away!'' Liddy blurted. ''I hate you.''

From the doorway Lori said, shocked, ''Liddy, I won't have you talking that way to Cade.''

Liddy banged her mug down on her little desk and flung herself on the bed. ''I hate you, too. You sent my daddy away!''

For an instant Lori looked as though someone had struck her across the face. Then she said steadily, ''Your father left because he wanted to. When you've calmed down, Liddy, I'll come back and talk to you. In the meantime, please stay in your room.''

Her shoulders sagging in her purple T-shirt, Lori trailed along the hall to the kitchen, sat down at the table and put her head in her hands. ''I just don't know what to *do*,'' she said in a muffled voice. ''I thought as you

and I saw more of each other, Cade, she'd come around.
But if anything, she's getting worse."

"Maybe we should cool it. Not see each other for a
while," Cade said tightly.

Her head jerked up. "Is that what you want?"

"For God's sake, no! But I hate seeing you pulled
two ways like this."

"I won't allow a five-year-old to dictate my life,"
Lori said wildly. "This weekend I'll sit down with her
and tell her what was going on between me and Ray.
His violence. His affair with Charlene. Even the way he
cheated my dad out of money. I should have done it
sooner, I've been letting her live in a dreamworld."

"You'll be destroying her innocence," Cade said
painfully.

"Yes...welcome to the real world, little Liddy," Lori
said with deep bitterness. "Under it all, I feel so guilty.
If I hadn't married such a horrible man, none of this
would have happened."

"If you hadn't married Ray you wouldn't have had
Liddy. So you're right, none of this would have happened."

She gave him a reluctant smile. "I guess you're
right."

All of a sudden Cade had had enough. Of Liddy, of
his unfulfilled hunger for Lori, and his own locked
tongue. "I'm going to get out of here," he said, "I
should do some more work on Sam's books. Why don't
we have lunch at the cafeteria tomorrow?"

"Okay," Lori said dispiritedly. He noticed how she
made no attempt to kiss him as he headed for the door,
and felt fear tighten his belly. If it came right down to
a choice between him and Liddy, what would she do?

She'd choose Liddy. She'd have to, despite all her
brave talk. Because she was Liddy's mother.

This wasn't a comforting conclusion. Cade went to

the garage, shut himself in the office and forced himself to concentrate. He was still there four hours later when the telephone rang. He picked up the receiver, hoping it was Lori; no one else knew he was here. But it wasn't Lori. A woman's voice said, "I'm looking for Cade MacInnis, please."

"Speaking."

"Mr. MacInnis, I'm calling from the hospital. You're listed as Samuel Withrod's next of kin, is that correct?"

Cade hadn't known Sam thought of him that way. But what had his old mentor said? *You're like a son to me.* Cade said tautly, "Yes. What's wrong?"

"Mr. Withrod's had a heart attack, he was admitted three hours ago. He's doing quite well, although he'll be in Coronary ICU until tomorrow...I'm glad I was able to track you down."

"I'll be right there," Cade said, jammed down the phone and ran for his car. He had to sign in at the intensive care ward; his nerves on edge, he walked over to Sam's bed.

His first thought was that Sam had shrunk; his second that Sam's face and the pillowcase were the identical shade of white. His third thought was achingly simple. *I love you, Sam...why did I never tell you that?*

There was a chair by the side of the bed. Cade sank down into it, his eyes glued to the other man's face, and rested his hand over Sam's, which was lying passively on the covers. With all his willpower and without uttering a sound he urged Sam to live. For Sam's sake. But also for his, Cade's.

Cade sat there for a long time. Nurses came by, doing things of which he was scarcely aware; he lost track of time and even of his surroundings, immersing himself in all his memories of Sam over the years, of Sam's joviality, his many kindnesses and his steady affection. And through it all ran the lament that he, Cade, had never told Sam how he felt about him.

He went home about four in the morning, had a shower and a sandwich, and went back to the hospital. The monitors clicked and bleeped, wavy green lines traced their mysterious patterns across the screens and Sam lay utterly still through it all. At eight-thirty when the doctors were doing their rounds, Cade was asked to leave; he stumbled into the hallway, dazed with tiredness, and remembered he'd agreed to meet Lori for lunch. He phoned the garage first, told Miguel what had happened and said he'd be in later. Then he phoned Lori.

Her voice sounded as fresh and immediate as if she were standing beside him, and for a moment his exhausted brain tricked him into wishing that she were. He said without a trace of emotion, "I'm at the hospital. Sam had a heart attack last night. They say he's doing well, although he's still in ICU."

And he looks as frail as a man ten years his senior. But Cade didn't say that; didn't admit to any of his fears or regrets.

"Oh Cade...how long have you been there?"

The sympathy in her voice nearly undid him; in reaction he sounded crushingly cold and formal. "Midnight, maybe, I don't really remember. I won't be able to meet you for lunch today, that's why I called."

"Of course, I understand. What kind of heart attack?"

Cade repeated all the technical jargon that one of the nurses had told him at two in the morning when she'd had some free time. None of it had meant very much, and he was aware of Lori's silence when he'd finished. Only wanting to be off the phone, he said, "I'd better go. I'll call you this evening if there's any news."

It was a relief to put down the receiver. He paced up and down the hallway for the next fifteen minutes, went back to sit by Sam's bed when the phalanx of interns and residents had filed out, and with an inward judder saw that Sam's eyes were open. In a feeble rasp Sam said, "Well, now, this is one place to hide from them tax fellers."

Cade managed a smile. "Kind of a drastic way of doing it."

"You don't look so hot."

"I feel a whole lot better for hearing your voice, you old son of a gun." Again Cade covered Sam's hand with his own, and the words came out surprisingly easily. "I realized something in the middle of the night, Sam...that I've never told you I love you. Past time I did."

Sam looked both highly discomfited and extremely touched. "Thanks, boy," he said huskily, and his eyes drifted shut.

As a couple of white-coated specialists sauntered over to Sam's bed, Cade was again ousted from his chair. He went out into the hall, all his emotions rising in his chest in an unstoppable tide; the pale pink paint and the varnished doors blurred in his vision. Desperate for privacy, he saw a door labeled Family Room, and lunged toward it. It was, to his infinite relief, empty. He sat down on the first chair he came to, and buried his head in his hands. From a long way away he heard a sob tear at his throat, then another, the hard, difficult sobs of a man who hadn't wept since he was a small boy.

Then, dimly, Cade became aware of something else. A woman's perfume, arms wrapping themselves around him, a voice saying his name over and over again. The perfume he recognized, the voice he would have known anywhere. Holding him with all her strength, Lori whispered, "Did Sam die?"

Cade shook his head. "It's not that," he choked. "I know I shouldn't be—"

"Yes, you should," she interrupted fiercely, "you've got a lifetime of tears locked up inside you, Cade," and let her cheek rest on his downbent head, her hands rhythmically stroking the tight muscles of his spine.

Cade didn't weep for long; but when it was over, he felt almost as though he were floating, as though a huge weight that he hadn't even known was resting on his shoulders had lifted itself and disappeared. He said hoarsely, "I don't want Sam to die, Lori…not like my dad."

With a careful lack of emphasis Lori said, "Did your father have a heart attack?"

"Yeah…I wasn't there, I'd gone to the station to pick up some parts that had come in on the train, so he died all alone on the gas station floor. Ten minutes later and I'd have been back. Sometimes I hated him, God knows…but I would never have wanted him to die by himself like that."

"You loved him, too."

"Of course I did." He swiped his face on the sleeve of his shirt. "I love Sam, too. I told him so half an hour ago…all night I was afraid I'd left it too late, that he'd die before I could tell him. Sam was the father I'd always wanted, steady and reliable, solid as a rock, and how's that for disloyalty?"

"It sounds natural enough to me. Why do you think I married Ray so young? Because I wanted to get away from my father, of course. Although I was much too immature to understand that."

"Neither of our fathers did well by us, did they?"

"Not really."

"I used to hate him when he was drunk," Cade said violently. "He changed personalities, he got slobbery and sentimental, and I never knew which was the real man. That one, or the man who could dance like Fred Astaire, was twice as charming and three times as aloof, and wouldn't tell you he loved you because that would have been an embarrassing display of emotion. Not cool.''

"Definitely not cool. Real instead," Lori snorted.

"I wasn't very old when I realized that if I didn't cover for him at the garage, he'd lose the franchise and be out of work. So we switched roles. I looked after him, instead of the other way around. I'm sure that was one reason I took off right after he died. To be footloose. To go where the wind blew me. Not responsible for anyone but myself."

Now that Cade's tongue was unlocked, it didn't want to stop. He told Lori in all its nasty detail about the bullying in the school yard, then about his mother's martyred attitude toward her marriage, and the three magical fishing trips he'd had with his dad when for over six months Dan MacInnis hadn't touched a drop of alcohol. Finally he said with a wry twist to his lips, "He didn't like you, he thought you were stuck-up."

"I was."

She was still crouched beside him, her eyes trained on his face. He said, "Maybe you were then. But you sure aren't now. And I'm running off at the mouth, I don't know what came over me...you don't want to listen to all this."

"You couldn't be more wrong!"

"I've never talked to anyone about my dad, what's the point? Lori, your knees must be killing you. Here, stand up."

Cade got up from the chair, pulling her to her feet so she was standing in the circle of his arms. He'd talked more than enough for one morning and Liddy wasn't anywhere in the vicinity. It seemed the most natural thing in the world to kiss Lori, covering her mouth with his own, breathing in the fragrance of her skin, and feeling along the length of his body the softness and warmth of her own. His kiss deepened, his tongue parting her lips, his arms straining her closer. "I never want to let you go," he muttered. "Sorry I dumped all that on you."

"*Sorry?* Cade, don't you *see?*" Lori said with exasperated intensity. "That's exactly what I do want from you—it's what I need. You talking to me. Telling me stuff. Real stuff. Intimate stuff. All about your feelings." She looked at him through her lashes. "Goodness, a man talking about his feelings...how very revolutionary."

"You don't want much, do you?"

"I want the real you. Not the macho mask, they're thick on the street." Her smile was very sweet; his head was swimming from more than worry and lack of sleep. "When Sam's well enough," she finished, "I'm going to tell him he did us a big favor."

Cade ran his fingertip along the line of her jaw, tracing the hard bone, absorbing through his pores the silkiness of her skin. "What made you come here?"

She gave a sudden chuckle. "First, to find out how Sam was. Second, if he was all right, to run up one side of you and down the other. You talked to me on the phone as if I was a complete stranger. Or one of those awful women who's nothing but a blathering nuisance and you can't wait to get rid of her. I decided you and I were overdue for a fight, and I was quite prepared to be the one to instigate it."

He tugged at her curls. "So despite Liddy and my own stubbornness, you're not ready to give up on me."

"Not yet," she said amicably. "But don't push your luck."

There was one more thing he had to say. "Lori, if it came to a choice between me and Liddy, you'd have to choose Liddy, I do see that."

In a thin whisper she said, "Then we mustn't let it get to that point, Cade."

Because she loved him? Somehow he didn't have the

courage to ask that particular question, not when his own feelings were in such confusion. And hadn't he said enough for one morning? "I'll try and talk to her the next time I see her."

"I just found out she's invited to a party on Saturday, it's her best friend from school. So I guess I shouldn't tell her about Ray on the weekend." Lori pulled a face. "Or am I just chickening out?"

"It'll work out somehow," Cade said; and knew how deeply he wanted to believe his own words.

She glanced at her watch and made a tiny exclamation of dismay. "I've got to go, I'm due at the gym in half an hour."

"I'll walk you to the door."

He put his hand under her elbow and kept it there down the corridor, in the elevator and out to the entrance. There she turned to face him. "Will you go to the garage today?"

He nodded. "I'll go back to ICU and find out what the specialists had to say. Then I'll head over there."

"Why don't you come for supper tonight?"

The sun was lying warm on the concrete sidewalk, and somewhere in the maples that edged the lawn a robin was singing the same phrase, over and over again. Cade said abruptly, "D'you know how I feel? As though I've stripped myself naked in front of you. Exposed myself to you...hell, Lori, I'm so tired I'm not making any sense. Forget it."

"It's what I've wanted you to do all along," she said in a low voice. "Please don't regret it, Cade!"

She wasn't running away because he'd longed for a father like Sam, and at times had ferociously resented his own father. The very opposite, in fact. In that little room across from the intensive care ward Cade was beginning to understand that he'd entered a whole new arena when it came to relationships: the difference between fixing a motorbike or an eighteen-wheeler. He mumbled, "Disoriented, that's how I feel."

She said slowly, "There's making love, that's one way to achieve intimacy...sometimes I think our whole culture revolves around that particular occupation. But then there's telling all your secrets and fantasies and longings to another person, the things you're ashamed of and that you've kept to yourself all your life. That's a much less acceptable route."

"Making love doesn't always bring intimacy. Look at you and Ray."

"Mmm...spilling your guts does, though. If it goes both ways. Although it's much harder."

Wanting to bring a smile to her face, Cade said, "Harder? Bad pun after that last kiss."

She answered loftily, "I should have said more difficult and I'm not blushing, it's just that the sun's warm."

"I love it when you blush," he said truthfully. "But, Lori, I've been a loner all my life—I can't change that overnight."

"Watch it, I might interpret that as a challenge," she said, a gleam in her eye. "There's my bus, I must run. Call me later." She pressed a quick kiss to his lips and ran down the curved driveway.

She ran as though she loved running; she was as fleet and graceful as the white-tailed deer that used to linger in the woods behind his father's garage in winter. She leaped up the stairs of the bus and the doors closed behind her. Cade walked back to the elevator.

The head nurse informed him that Sam was to be moved to a regular ward that morning; he was well on his way to recovery. "He should treat this heart attack as a wake-up call," she said briskly. "He needs to exercise more, cut out the fish and chips and quit worrying about his income tax. See what you can do about all that, hmm?''

Sam in the weight room? It seemed about as likely as Liddy giving Cade a hug. "Right," Cade said. "Can I see him again before I go?"

"Ten minutes."

As soon as Cade went in the door, Sam said, "There you are, boy, 'bout time. Listen, you got to keep an eye on Joel, he's fine on VW's but not so great on Mazdas, and we got a run on Mazdas for some reason…and on Monday an Alfa Romeo's booked, you look after that yourself, you hear? Don't let anyone else near it. Then on Tuesday when Miguel—"

"Sam," Cade said forcefully, "shut your trap." Sam gave a squawk like a startled crow. Cade went on, "I won't bankrupt you, I won't let anyone else as much as breathe on the Alfa Romeo, and I'll keep an eye on all the guys. If you don't trust me, why'd you make me your partner?"

"Not saying I don't trust you," Sam huffed.

"Yes, you are. The garage'll be fine, I'm going there right now and I won't leave until I'm sure everything's under control…worrying like this is one reason why you're here. Give it a rest, huh?"

"I'll be outta here in no time."

"And there'll be some changes when you do get out," Cade announced. "I'll get the last of the accounting on the computer this weekend, so you don't have to sweat that anymore. You're going to start walking to work every day. And I'm going to tell the diner across the street they're not to serve you as much as a French fry. Let alone fish deep-fried in batter."

"You're my partner, not my mother!"

"For the next while I'm your boss. And don't you forget it. Now take care of yourself, you old coot, and I'll be in to see you tonight." Cade added gruffly, "I want you to be bugging me for a long while to come, you got that?''

"Yeah...thanks, boy."

Cade strode out of the room. If he didn't watch out, he'd be blubbering again like a baby. Feelings were all very well. But what when they got out of hand? And once you'd let them out, how did you shove them back where they belonged?

As a more or less direct result of that thought he left a message on Lori's answering machine, saying he wouldn't go for supper, he had too much work at the garage. Which, he knew, was both true and untrue, and merely delayed the moment when they would be together again; when he'd discover if he was going to backslide into the taciturnity that had served him for so long, or if he'd continue babbling like the brook that used to run between his father's gas station and the Presbyterian church.

He knew which of these alternatives Lori wanted; she'd left him in no doubt about that. But when he'd told her he felt naked and exposed, he'd spoken the truth. He didn't like feeling that way; it was a whole lot more dangerous than tackling six bullies in an alleyway.

Cade worked very hard all that day and well into the evening. He grabbed a couple of hamburgers for supper, glad Sam couldn't see him devouring what must be pure cholesterol. Afterward he organized the bookings for Monday and Tuesday, deciding that computerizing those would be his next innovation; although he'd probably have to give Sam time to get used to the idea. On the weekend he'd do the payroll and read up on Alfa Romeos.

Cade went back to his apartment about eleven, his head swimming with tiredness. His answering machine was blinking. Lori's warm contralto surged into the room. "Cade, do you know what I'd like to do? Go out to French Bay tomorrow afternoon. Rachel's got soccer practice then she's going to the movies, and Liddy's at her party. So I could go around four.'' Suddenly she sounded uncertain. ''If you'd like to, that is.''

It was too late to phone her tonight. If he took her to French Bay, he'd want to make love to her...not that French Bay had the exclusive rights on that particular need. He could happily have made love to her this morning on the lawn outside the hospital. Or in the empty room next to Sam's. That would have given the specialists something to talk about.

I'll decide tomorrow, thought Cade, fell into bed and didn't wake up until ten past ten.

Lori wasn't home when he phoned. ''I'll pick you up at four. I'll be at the garage if there's any change,'' he said into her answering machine and jammed down the receiver. Trouble was, he wouldn't be taking a disembodied voice to French Bay, he'd be taking Lori. Who definitely came with a body.

If he was going to accomplish anything this morning, he'd better keep his mind off Lori Cartwright's delectable and desirable body.

Did he only want what he couldn't see his way clear to having?

CHAPTER TEN

LORI was waiting for Cade when he arrived at her apartment. She was wearing jeans and a baggy fuschia sweater over a white shirt; he dragged his eyes away from the curve of her hip as she climbed in the car. "Hi, Lori, how are you?"

Scintillating opening, buddy. Better that if you can.

"Fine." She busied herself with the seat belt. "I hope you didn't mind me asking to go to French Bay, I've got a yen to be by the sea and it's not very often both girls are gone at the same time and for so long, I feel like it's a mini-vacation, are you sure it's all right?"

"So you're nervous. Me, too."

"Except you don't show it," she said tartly.

She'd bundled some of her hair into a clip on the back of her head; the rest hung in soft curls against her neck. She smelled luscious. "I was a damn fool to give you that perfume," he muttered, pulling out on the street.

"But I love it!"

He'd like to leave a trail of it from her breasts down her belly to her thighs, then follow that trail with his mouth. Which wasn't something he could very well share with her. "How are the girls?"

She chattered on about Rachel's excellent mark in science and disgraceful mark in French, and how Marvin had taken to sleeping on Liddy's pillow at night. Then she said, "I had a letter from Ray yesterday. He doesn't want me writing to him again, and he's much too busy to see the girls or write to them. A clean break is much the best thing, wouldn't I agree, yours, Ray." Absorbedly she traced the side seam of her jeans with

135

her nail. "How do I explain that one to Rachel and Liddy?"

"Rachel's already worked it out. Liddy's very busy denying it. Maybe, eventually, you show her the letter."

"I'll talk to her next weekend," Lori said, now digging at the seam. "At least that gives her a couple of days home, so perhaps she and I can thrash it out somehow."

Gently Cade lifted her hand, transferring it to his lap. "Don't do that, you'll wear out the stitching."

The heat of her palm soaked through his jeans; luckily his sweater had stretched in the wash, hiding his body's instant and irrefutable response. I'll go mad if I don't make love to this woman soon, he thought. Maybe if I take it slow, treat her like a piece of fragile crystal. Or like one of those poppies whose petals bruise if you brush against them…maybe then she wouldn't mind too much.

He knew about control…hadn't he been controling his sexuality for years? He should be able to handle Lori just fine.

To fill a silence that felt as loud as his mother's when his dad would come home drunk, Cade told her quite a lot about the doings at the garage, and then described his visit with Sam that morning. "He's definitely feeling better. Asking all the specialists what kind of cars they drive, ordering the nurses around and me along with them. He walked the length of the corridor after breakfast and he says the food's lousy."

They were out of town now. Cade speeded up, his arm resting on the window ledge, the wind tousling his hair. "I'm arranging for someone to come in and cook and clean for him when he gets home. Haven't told him that yet. The garage floor's cleaner than his kitchen."

Lori asked some questions, and before Cade was quite ready for it they were driving through the spruce trees that led toward the house. "Want to walk along the shore?" he asked. That would be safe. There were too many houses on the opposite shore for him to get into any trouble.

"I need to use the bathroom," she said stiffly. "Will you let me in?"

The house, as always, welcomed Cade. As Lori disappeared upstairs he opened some windows, because the ceramic tile had just been laid in the kitchen and he could still smell the glue. They'd done a great job, though; he'd enjoy cooking in this kitchen.

"Cade," Lori called, "could you come up here, please?"

Her voice sounded unusually tense. He took the stairs two at a time, and found her standing in his bedroom beside the futon with its patchwork quilt. Her eyes were huge, her hands deep in her pockets, pulling her jeans even tighter to her thighs; her shoulders were hunched. "Lori," he said, "what's the matter?"

"I had a very classy speech all planned, but I seem to have forgotten it." She gulped, scuffing at the floor with her toe.

He had no idea where she was coming from. "I don't need classy speeches. Just tell me what's wrong, I hate to see you looking so worried."

Taking a deep breath, Lori gabbled, "I'm doing just what I did ten years ago—throwing myself at you. With about as much finesse. I want to make love to you, that's what I'm trying to say. Now. Here. Today."

Cade couldn't, for the life of him, come up with a reply. His face felt congealed; all her own tension had transferred itself to him. She wasn't joking, though. That much was obvious.

Something else was glaringly obvious. Her technique was very different from ten years ago. Then she'd worn a sweater so tight he'd wondered how she could breathe, with a neckline that plunged into her cleavage; her mini-skirt had economized on fabric and her legs had seemed to go on forever. She'd thrown herself at him quite literally, rubbing against him, kissing him with a breathy inexpertise that had made him dizzy with desire. But today, in jeans and a bulky sweater, she was positioned two feet away from him and looked as though a seductive move was the farthest thing from her mind.

She looked, if truth were told, as if she were standing in front of a firing squad; she was staring at him, her cheeks as pale as moments ago they had been pink. In a hollow voice she said, "Oh God. You don't want to. I've blown it."

With a whimper of pure distress she tried to run past him for the stairs. But Cade, acting automatically, caught her by the sleeve. "Let go!" she cried. "I'm sorry, I shouldn't have said anything. But ever since I told you about Ray you've been avoiding me, you backed right off and I couldn't bear it, it's been driving me crazy. So I thought I'd just ask you, right out, to go to bed with me. I shouldn't have, I see that now, it was an awful mistake, as many feet as a centipede and all in my mouth at once, why do I keep *doing* that? Cade, let's go for a walk on the shore and look at the waves and for heaven's sake forget I ever said a word." She tugged frenziedly at her arm. "Will you *please* let go of me!"

"Lori," Cade said in a voice that seemed to come from the next room, "I want to."

"You don't have to—" She broke off, looking up at him. "Want to what?"

His tongue felt as thick as the quilt on the bed. "Make love to you, of course—what else?"

"No, you don't, I can tell that you don't. History's repeating itself—you're turning me down. Although rather more politely than last time, I do have to say."

"I'm not turning you down!" He rubbed at his face

with his free hand. "I want to make love to you so badly I can hardly breathe. I can't sleep, I dream about you all the time, and the only way I've been able to keep my hands off you is by remembering what Ray did to you."

"You don't know how often I've regretted telling you that!"

"You had to tell me. You couldn't pretend it didn't happen."

"Then why have you been treating me like I'm a total turnoff ever since?" she demanded furiously.

The truth, Cade. You've done it before, you can do it again. "Remember how you screamed? Right in this room? When I threw myself on top of you on the bed?" He let go of her arm, purposely increasing the distance between them. "Any time I'd think of making love with you, I'd hear that scream again. I was so scared of frightening you that I backed off altogether."

"You were *afraid?*"

"Of course I was. I wouldn't hurt you for the world."

"Oh." She produced a travesty of a smile. "I thought you didn't want me anymore. Used goods and all that."

Appalled, he exclaimed, "Lori!"

"Why didn't you *tell* me?"

"I should have. I didn't know how…men aren't supposed to be scared of stuff like that." Desperate to convince her, Cade added, "I can be gentle—I'll treat you like glass if that's what it takes, I swear I will. But if I don't soon take you to bed, I'll go out of my mind."

Her face unreadable, Lori said, "So you're not turning me down."

"No." Belatedly his brain started to function. "Although I don't have anything to protect you against pregnancy."

"I'm still on the Pill because of irregularities in my cycle." She looked at him helplessly. "Now what do we do?"

"You're sure you want to?"

She swallowed, her throat moving convulsively. Was she having second thoughts, Cade wondered, now that she'd gotten what she'd asked for? "Yes," she whispered, "yes, I want to."

His heart was thumping in his chest as loudly as the rock music in an aerobics class; but he knew exactly what he had to do. It was up to him, now. Lori was trusting him to look after her, and not for all her father's money would he fail her. He knelt and pulled back the quilt on the makeshift bed on the floor; then he shucked off his deck shoes, put his arms around her and began kissing her with infinite tenderness and all the skill at his disposal, every movement as leisurely as the sun's slow drift across the polished floorboards.

What he wasn't quite prepared for was Lori's response. Only for a fraction of a minute was she rigid in his embrace; then she swayed toward him, her hands circling his waist and drawing him closer, her mouth opening as flower petals open to the sun. Easy, he told himself, take it easy. But of its own accord his tongue circled her lips, probed deeper, met her own in a dance that seemed to melt the bones in his body.

He was instantly and fully aroused. Rather than pulling her against him, as instinct cried out for him to do, he concentrated on letting his lips drift over her face, his fingers buried in her soft, clustered curls. I knew that perfume would get me into trouble, he thought dimly, and remembered his fantasy of dripping it between her breasts, following it all the way to the juncture of her thighs.

He couldn't rush her; she deserved better of him than that. But the soft urgency of her lips inflamed his senses; he caressed the slope of her shoulders, feeling through the fluffy mohair her angled collarbones and the firmness of muscle. She slid her palms from his scalp to his own shoulders, then down his chest, and for a moment broke free of his kisses, her smudged blue eyes full of questions.

Cade said unsteadily, "Are you okay?"

"A lot more okay than I was when I called you upstairs," she said with a breathless laugh.

"I can't quite believe this is happening. You and I about to make love together. After all these years."

She blurted, "Cade, are *you* okay?"

"Oh yes," he said, "for sure."

His obvious sincerity must have encouraged her. She said, "For all my fine talk about intimacy and sex, I feel as though I've never done this before. There's never been anyone but Ray, I told you that, and you and he are so different..."

Maximizing that difference was precisely why Cade was struggling to maintain his self-control. "You're safe with me," he murmured, nuzzling the slim line of her throat, achingly aware of her fingers clasping his nape and playing with his hair. It wouldn't matter what she did; her every move fired his hunger for her and made his struggle all the more difficult. When he kissed her again, her pliancy was its own message. Emboldened, he slid his hands between her sweater and her shirt. With a quiver of laughter he muttered, "No bra...so you were planning ahead."

She was nibbling at his lips, punctuating this with little bursts of words. "I had to...I didn't know what else to do...and it worked, didn't it?"

"Indeed it did," he said, and eased the sweater over her head. Her nipples were pushing against the white cotton of her shirt. He cupped her flesh in his hands, glorying in its swelling warmth, in her sharp, indrawn breath. Very deliberately, his eyes trained on her face, he began undoing the buttons on her shirt. They were small, hidden beneath a placket; for a man whose job depended on manual dexterity, he was being exceedingly inept.

When he reached the last one, he opened her shirt to bare her breasts, drinking in their ripe beauty. His expression must have changed; Lori said shakily, "Oh Cade..." and in sudden impatience tugged at his sweater. "I want to lie down with you," she said, "I want you to hold me..."

He flung his sweater to the floor, undoing his own shirt. "We've got all afternoon, sweetheart," he said, "there's no rush," and knew he was talking to himself as much as to her; knew, too, that he'd never been a man for casual endearments. He drew her toward him and with a shock of pure pleasure felt the soft weight of her breasts against his chest. Her face was burrowed into the hollow at the base of his throat, her hair tickling his chin. I've come home, Cade thought, and in a flare of panic wondered what the outcome of this lovemaking would be.

Then thought was engulfed in sensation as Lori rubbed herself in slow circles against him, her hips pushing themselves into his erection. He gasped her name, took her by the shoulders and gently pushed her away, lowering his head to explore the silken slopes of her breasts, the valley between them, and their taut, rosy tips. With huge gratification he heard her whimper with pleasure. Only then did he reach for the zipper on her jeans.

She helped him pull them down her hips along with her lacy underwear, kicking off her shoes and yanking at her socks, until she stood naked before him. Her face was suddenly shy, deeply uncertain. She muttered, "I've had two children, Cade, I know it shows..."

"You think I mind?"

"It's marked me," she stumbled. "Ray always hated

it when I was pregnant. And afterward, too, when I breast-fed the girls.''

Ray again. So the damage done by Lori's ex-husband had gone much deeper than the physical; he'd made Lori, who used to be so supremely self-confident, doubt herself. Cade said, letting his burning gaze encompass her from head to foot, ''You're so beautiful you take my breath away.'' Then he reached out and traced the stretch marks on her belly with infinite tenderness, bringing his hands together over her navel. ''Your daughters are part of you,'' he said fiercely, ''and came from your body. These marks only add to your beauty, they couldn't possibly detract from it.''

''You really mean that?''

''Of course I do.''

Unconsciously she stood taller, her eyes bright with a new pride. ''That was part of the reason I was so afraid when I called you up here...that you'd find me unattractive. Undesirable.''

Cade threw back his head, his shout of laughter coming from deep in his chest and releasing some of his own tension. ''Oh Lori, you couldn't have been more wrong. Undesirable? I'd hate to have to describe some of the dreams I've been having about you.''

''You, too, eh?'' she said wickedly, and tugged at the waistband of his jeans. ''No fair. Me with no clothes on and you still dressed.''

He couldn't possibly hide the fact that his body was achingly ready for her; but although she looked both flustered and gratified, she didn't look afraid. He tossed his socks to the floor along with his jeans and briefs, and drew her down to lie beside him on the futon. The late afternoon sun gilded her body and through the window he heard the splash of the waves breaking on the rocks. ''You belong here,'' he said huskily, and set out to convince her just how much that was true; and just how very desirable he did find her.

But slowly, Cade. Slowly.

He didn't want to go slow. He wanted to sweep Lori into the turbulence that was surging, powerful as any sea, throughout his entire body. To ravish her, plunge into her and lay claim to her in the most primitive way he knew how.

Replacing Ray. Making her his own.

Instead Cade began kissing her again, reining himself in as tightly as he could. He stroked and caressed her at breast and flank and belly, listening for her response with more than his ears, sensing her impatience even though he was afraid to trust in it. Yet she was warm and wet to his touch when he opened her thighs; she writhed beneath his fingertips, her tiny cries like those of sandpipers on the shore.

He played with her, desperate for her, resting his weight on one elbow so he wouldn't crush her into the mattress. Her face was as naked to him as her body, suffused with the kind of pleasure that hovers on the boundary of pain, and suddenly Cade could wait no longer. His throat tight, he slid into her, feeling her envelop him as though this was indeed where he most truly belonged. He tried even then for restraint; but inexorably her silken clutch and his own strokes seized hold of him until he was powerless to resist. Lori cried out his name, once, twice; in fierce impulsion Cade found his release within her, fighting back the hoarse shout of completion that wanted to crowd its way from his lungs.

His back was slick with sweat. He felt drained and for some reason—he recognized the feeling with a shock of surprise—afraid. "Lori," he said softly, easing over onto his side and drawing her with him, "are you all right?"

Her heart was racing against his rib cage and she was

breathing in small gasps. For several long moments she lay in his embrace with her eyes closed. Her cheeks were washed with delicate color; her hands were clutching his shoulders, and the longer she remained silent, the more his fear burgeoned in his chest. Then she looked up. "Tell me the truth, Cade, because this is really important," she said. "You were holding back the whole time, weren't you? Because of Ray?"

He nodded, not trusting himself to speak. Tears glittered under her lids. "You didn't want to frighten me, so you kept yourself and your own needs in check...it's been so long since anyone's looked after me that I'd forgotten how amazing and wonderful it feels."

Uncomfortably Cade shifted on the mattress. "Don't make me into some kind of saint." His smile was ironic. "I've just proved I'm no ascetic."

With passionate intensity Lori said, "I'm so fortunate to have found you again. Because for the first time in months I really feel as though Ray's gone. Gone forever. You've driven the last remnants of him away by being so good to me, by putting my needs first."

Cade voiced the one thing that was clear among the roiling emotions in his chest. "I'm glad he's gone."

"You know what?" she said impulsively. "I think we need a repeat performance. And this time I want you to remember two things. I won't break. And I don't want you to hold back, not the slightest bit." She scowled in thought. "Make that three things. Take that famous control of yours and toss it out the window. We both deserve better."

To his faint embarrassment Cade felt his groin stir to life. Lori added pertly, "I can see you like my idea."

"I like it a lot," he growled. "Come here, woman, and I'll show you how much I like it."

He didn't have to hold back, ever again. Because Lori had set him free.

He twisted, covering her with his big frame, thrusting one thigh between hers and kissing her with all the pent-up hunger that their first lovemaking hadn't assuaged. Had, if anything, increased. She met him more than half-way, her hips moving below him in slow, sinuous circles, her nails digging into his spine, her tongue laving his lips and teeth. Deep within Cade, something too long caged broke free. Lori wanted him to be himself, that's what she was saying. To lose the control that had been with him for as long as he could remember.

Yes, he thought. Yes.

He took the tip of her breast between his lips, playing with it with a sensuality that mounted his body like an ocean tide, slowly, inexorably and powerfully. Then he rolled on his back, pulling her with him as he explored all the dips and hollows of her body with his hands and mouth. He forgot to be gentle and abandoned restraint, and to his wonderment realized his own wildness was releasing a matching wildness in her. Far from being afraid, Lori was liberated by the change in him. Exultant, he lifted her to straddle him, her knees clasping him by the hips, her breasts golden in the light.

Her face was intent as she rode him, her lower lip caught between her teeth. But before he could break, he lifted her again so that she lay flat on her back, her hair tangled on the pillow. "The perfume I bought you," he said, "I wanted to touch it to your breasts and your belly, and then follow it with my mouth. Here. And here. And then here."

She gasped with pleasure as his head slid lower and lower, rippling her fingers through his thick, dark hair. "Cade," she cried, "oh please...now."

He gave a jubilant laugh. "So you want me, Lori?"

She sat up in a single graceful flow of movement. "I've never wanted anyone the way I want you," she said. "But now it's my turn, Cade. Lie still."

Then she was all over him, teasing his body hair, caressing the hard jut of his pelvis, encircling the rigidity that was all his hunger for her. He shuddered to her touch, wondering if he would die with pleasure here in a house by the sea with a woman who had captured his heart so many years ago. A woman on whom he was now placing his seal.

He on her and she on him.

Taking her by the hips, he threw himself on top of her and plunged intð her, feeling her rise to gather him in, his thrusts more than matched by her own. His gaze was fastened on her face, watching every play of expression as her climax seized her and flung her toward him. He met her with deep joy and with all the passion that had been locked inside him for so long; and this time Cade heard his voice cry her name to the four walls and to the four winds of the sea.

He collapsed on top of her, his breath harsh in his throat. His chest was heaving as hard as it had that day he'd run around the park in an endeavor to forget her. As for Lori, she was utterly quiescent; he looked into her eyes and saw his own wonder and satiation reflected there. "Dearest Lori," he said and pulled her close, holding her as if he never wanted to let her go.

Stroking her hair back from her face, dropping little kisses on her forehead, he murmured, "I spent a summer on the prairies years ago...your hair reminds me of the grain fields. They went for miles, waving in the wind like a sea of gold. One day I threw myself down in the wheat, lay on my back and felt the sun on my face, my nostrils filled with ripeness...that's how you make me feel. Sunlight and ripeness and the heat of summer."

"Nobody's ever said anything like that to me before," Lori whispered. "You don't talk often, Cade. But when you do, you say something so beautiful that I—" Suddenly she wrapped her arms so tightly around him that he could scarcely breathe. "Hold on to me. Just hold on and don't let go."

Cade gathered her even closer; not for the first time, he was aware of a burning anger toward Ray. For what Lori was revealing, intentionally or otherwise, was the desert her marriage had been. Barren of love and the golden ripeness of wheat, destitute of laughter and passion.

Eventually her arms slackened their hold; the rhythm of her breathing told him she'd fallen asleep. The thigh that was lying under her was cramped, as was his right arm. But not for anything would Cade have moved.

He was glad they'd made love for the first time in his house by the sea. Lori's deliciously wanton response to his lovemaking had filled him with a wholly male pride; it had also filled him with humility. For he, Cade MacInnis, had been able to free Lori from the past. Right here in this room he'd brought her both happiness and fulfillment.

He rested his cheek on her hair and lay still.

CHAPTER ELEVEN

Two hours later Cade and Lori were back in her apartment. Lori looked around the kitchen, holding to her chest one of the bags of groceries they'd picked up on the way home. "I feel as though I've been away forever," she said. "As though I'm not the same woman who left here."

He took the bag from her, put it on the table and kissed her thoroughly. "You taste the same," he said.

She giggled, rubbed herself very explicitly against his blue jeans and said extravagantly, "I adore the way you taste, Cade. Actually, I adore everything about your body."

"If the girls weren't due back in fifteen minutes, guess where we'd be."

"Making love in the refrigerator?"

He put his hands to her waist and lifted her over his head, laughing up at her. "Oh, I might manage to restrain myself long enough to pull you to the floor." As he lowered her, she wrapped her thighs around his hips, rocking against him. His breath hissed between his teeth. "I can't get enough of you," he muttered and kissed her again.

The buzzer sounded. Startled, he dropped Lori to the floor. She pressed the button to let Rachel in and said faintly, "Why are children never late when you want them to be?"

"Don't ask me," said Cade, grabbed the nearest bag of groceries and started stacking things haphazardly on the kitchen table.

She added hurriedly, "Cade, please don't take this

wrong but I don't think you can stay here overnight. Because of Rachel and Liddy. Liddy, mostly.''

She was right, of course. And how he hated it. He said, as evenly as he could, ''We'll figure something out, don't—''

Rachel banged on the door. Lori let her in, following her into the kitchen. Rachel cried, ''Guess what, Mum? The coach has picked me to go with the team to Windsor next Saturday morning, will you come and watch us play? You could come, too, Cade, that'd be neat, I miss having a father who goes to games and stuff. And the movie was great, it was all about this girl called Matilda who liked to read, just like me—oh yum, are we having steak for supper?''

''Yes, we are,'' said Cade, and wondered if the word father was ringing in Lori's ears as it was in his own. He didn't know anything about being a father. But he could learn...couldn't he?

He said, laying claim to Lori's living space as earlier he had laid claim to her body, ''Lori, if you put the groceries away, I'll start supper.''

She gaped at him. ''What?''

Rachel glanced from one to the other. ''What's up? You look funny, Mum.''

''Do I? I can't imagine why,'' Lori babbled. ''Put your gear in your room, darling, before I trip on it.''

Rachel said, and only the slightest quiver in her voice showed how important this was to her, ''I'd like it a lot if you were my new father, Cade.''

''Rachel!'' Lori exclaimed.

The little girl's face fell. ''Well, I would,'' she said obstinately. ''I just wish Liddy'd smarten up, she's being really dumb. Besides, then you wouldn't have to worry about money so much, Mum. We could have steak all the time.''

Rachel wasn't going to give up, Cade realized, not

until she had an answer. But he didn't need this kind of pressure. It was too soon; he hadn't had the chance to assimilate a lovemaking unlike any other in his life, let alone map out the future. Sounding brusque even to his own ears, he said, "Rachel, your mum and I haven't been dating for very long, so it's not appropriate to be talking about me being a stepfather."

"I don't see why not."

Striving for honesty, he added, "I'm complimented that you think of me that way, though."

With some of her mother's tenacity Rachel blurted, "Don't you want to marry my mum?"

"We're not in love with each other—so that's not a question I can answer," Cade said bluntly; and heard his own words echo in his head. For a fleeting second he allowed himself to wonder what it would be like to be married to Lori. "But your mother's a lovely woman, Rachel, and I'm very glad she and I are friends."

"Friends," Lori repeated in an unreadable voice. "Yes. Your gear, please, Rachel."

Rachel lifted her blue sports bag off the floor. Her brow was furrowed. "Does the guy still have to do the asking?" she said. "Or can you, Mum?"

Lori's cheeks were aflame; Cade was sure she was remembering how only a few hours ago she was the one who had indeed done the asking. But she'd asked him to make love to her, not marry her. He said hastily, "It can go either way. Off you go, Rachel," and tried not to notice how naturally he'd taken authority over her.

As Rachel left the room, dragging her bag, Lori turned her back and started shoving groceries into the refrigerator. Cade reached over and took a can of tomato paste out of her hand. "That goes in the cupboard, not the freezer."

She faltered, "We've taken this huge step and now I don't know what to do."

"We don't have to do anything," he said, and watched her lashes lower to hide her eyes. "Except get a baby-sitter as often as possible so you can sleep in *my* bed."

"I can't stay overnight, though." As she pushed a Romaine lettuce onto the bottom shelf, a bag of carrots tumbled to the floor. "Oh *damn*," she exclaimed.

Something had upset her. But what? Had she disliked the way he'd dealt with Rachel? But what other choice had he had?

Before Cade could formulate any of these questions, the buzzer sounded again. "That'll be Liddy," Lori said, grimacing.

Cade pushed the button and a few moments later opened the door. Liddy gave him an unfriendly look. He said, "Hello, Liddy."

"Hello," she said and scurried into the kitchen. "Mum, look what I got at the party, and I swam the whole length of the pool all by myself."

After she had shown her mother her candy and toys, she went off to hang her swimsuit in the bathroom. Cade said, "If you and Rachel do the dishes after supper, I'll see if I can have a talk with Liddy."

"Why bother?" Lori said coldly. "You told Rachel it was inappropriate to be thinking about the future."

He could feel his temper rising. "Lori, when I go out the door tonight I'm not going to disappear, will you get that through your head? Consequently, I'd much prefer if your younger daughter and I were on speaking terms."

"Do you want a salad with the steak?"

"Yes," said Cade, kissed her hard on the mouth and bent to get the broiler from the bottom of the stove. He hated the way those magical hours at French Bay had retreated so quickly. Even Lori had retreated from him. Maybe she didn't want him anywhere near her children. It wasn't as though he was an expert on kids, after all.

Or maybe she was angry that he'd so easily found his way into Rachel's affections; angry at him, too, for upsetting Liddy.

He'd be better with Rachel and Liddy than his own father had been with him, or Morris Campbell with his daughter Lorraine. Better by far. So who was she to judge?

Considering his level of preoccupation, Cade cooked a more than creditable supper, and afterward, when Rachel and Lori were busy at the sink, he walked down the hall. Liddy was in the living room, coloring in the new book that she'd been given at the party. He sat down beside her on the carpet. "Liddy, I want to tell you a story. I know you resent me going out with your mum—but I'd just like you to listen for a few minutes."

Picking at a loose thread in his sock, he said, "When I was a little boy the same age as you, I had a dad and a mum. But my dad liked to drink too much beer and wine, and he wouldn't pay the bills or go to work or look after me the way a father should. When he drank too much he'd walk funny and sing silly songs on the street, so the kids at school used to make fun of me. I hated it. Sometimes I hated him and wished I could have normal parents like everybody else."

Industriously Liddy colored Snow White's dress red, her crayon digging into the paper. Choosing his words, Cade said, "I'm telling you this so you'll know I understand what it's like not to have a proper father. To miss him. I'll do my best to be good to your mother, Liddy. To you and Rachel, too."

He seemed to have run out of words. Liddy put down the red and picked up green. She said, "My daddy doesn't drink too much."

"No. But when my dad drank, it was as though he'd gone away. Like your dad has."

Liddy's crayon made jagged streaks all over the hillside behind Snow White; a tear plopped onto the page. Cade put his hand on her shoulder. "I'm really sorry you miss your dad so much."

For a brief moment she leaned into his hand, and with a surge of hope Cade thought he'd gotten through to her. But then she said mutinously, "I don't want another daddy."

Cade wasn't about to enter that debate. He said, "Any time you want to talk about your father, I'm available," got up and went down the hall to the bathroom. His own face stared back at him in the mirror. Somehow he'd expected it to look different after everything that had happened that day.

He was sexually involved with a woman who had two daughters, one of whom wanted him to marry her mother, the other of whom couldn't stand the sight of him. What the mother wanted, he had no idea.

And what about himself? What did he want?

He wanted to take the mother back to bed. Now. That much he did know. Not that he was going to get it.

Nor did he. When the girls were both settled in their room, Lori said, "Cade, I'm really tired, I need an early night."

He said flatly, "Have I said or done something to offend you?"

"Not at all."

He wasn't going to suggest they get a sitter and go to his place so he could take her to bed there. She'd say no. He could tell. And he didn't like rejection any more than the next man.

But if only he could make love to her, he'd be able to break through the barrier that seemed to have arisen between them, a barrier whose origin he didn't understand but whose reality he was feeling in every nerve in his body.

Instead Cade contented himself with taking Lori in his

arms and kissing her, trying very hard not to let his frustration show. Her body was stiff in his embrace. She did kiss him back; but with none of the fervor she'd shown earlier. "Everything will work out, don't worry," he said, and saw how her kingfisher-blue eyes were shuttered against him. "Let's get together sometime tomorrow."

"What for?"

She looked as hostile as Liddy. "What do you mean—what for?" he retorted. "Do I have to analyze every move I make?"

"All you want to do is take me to bed."

With a huge effort Cade modulated his voice. "That's not true and you know it. Why don't I come over in the afternoon? Maybe we could all go to the museum."

Glowering at him, Lori said, "Fine."

"I'll visit Sam first. How about three-thirty?"

She nodded. He snapped, "You can't wait for me to go out that door, can you?"

"I need some time to myself!"

Suddenly it hit Cade what was wrong. Hit him like a blow. "You're sorry we made love, aren't you? You're wishing we never had."

"No! Of course not."

"I don't believe you."

"This afternoon in bed with you—it was wonderful. But it's like a dream now." Lori's eyes darted around the crowded little kitchen, whose walls were decorated with Rachel and Liddy's artwork. "This is reality."

The words came from deep within Cade, forcing themselves to the surface. "Lori, making love to you was the most real thing I've ever done in my whole life."

"Was it? Was it really?"

"I'm real, too, dammit!" He thrust out his arm. "Try me."

As if she couldn't help herself, Lori rested her bare fingers on his wrist, where the jagged white scar from his accident on the oil rig protruded from the sleeve of his sweater. He said, his mind not really on his words, "A half inch the other way, the doc said, and I'd have been a goner because the artery would have been severed...I was lucky."

She said, aghast, "Then you'd never have come back. To Nova Scotia. To me."

"Guess not."

"Oh Cade," she cried, throwing herself on his chest and burrowing her nose into his shoulder, "I'm sorry, I know I'm behaving like an idiot, I just don't know which way is up anymore. How can going to bed with you have done that to me?"

"That's a very complicated question," Cade said, and tipped up her face to kiss her again. This time Lori met him as eagerly as she had in his sunlit bedroom; his heart leaped in his chest like a kid let out of school. Against the soft curve of her lips he said, "Get a sitter tomorrow night."

"Yes," she breathed. "Would eight-thirty be too late?"

"Two minutes from now is too late," he growled and kissed her again. When they broke apart a few minutes later, she was panting and he was in no shape to be seen in a public place. He said unsteadily, "Sleep well, sweetheart," and watched a radiant smile illumine her features.

Cade let himself out, ran to his car and hummed tunelessly all the way back to his apartment, where he spent the better part of two hours cleaning, tidying, and laundering sheets and towels. He didn't think about the future, he refused to allow himself to worry about Liddy and he closed his mind to Lori's edginess. His happiness in the present moment was more than enough.

He slept like a dead man and woke up thinking of Lori. At the garage that morning he finished the accounts; at the hospital Sam looked like a different man, his face no longer sunken and pallid. He was also champing to go home. Cade took him to the cafeteria for a coffee, filling him in on the doings at the garage; as they walked back to the ward, Sam said, "You still got woman troubles?"

"Nope," said Cade. "Soon as you sign the pledge to steer clear of fish and chips, I'll introduce you to her."

"Humph," said Sam. "She's worth that?"

"Oh, she is," Cade said, "she is."

"Once every two weeks," Sam said craftily. "That wouldn't hurt me."

"Once a month."

"I'll think about it."

"You'll like her, Sam," Cade said. "She's Morris Campbell's daughter, from Juniper Hills. I've known her for years."

"You're aiming high."

"So's she," Cade grinned.

"I like your attitude," Sam said. "You take your time with that Alfa Romeo, you hear me?"

"Yessir," said Cade, and left Sam at the door of the ward. He then drove to Lori's.

When he knocked on her door, Lori opened it. After quickly checking that the kitchen was empty, he reached out for her. Evading him, she said in a voice higher-pitched than usual, "My mother's here, Cade, a surprise visit for a couple of days. My father's off on a business trip."

His disappointment was so acute that he felt as though someone had punched him hard in the stomach. "No sitter," he said. No lovemaking.

"No," she said expressionlessly. "We'll have to skip

the museum, too. But I told her you were invited for supper."

Cade grasped her by the wrist. "Aren't you disappointed?"

Lori glanced over her shoulder, then pulled his head down. Her kiss, while brief, was astonishingly comprehensive. She said, "That should—oh no, I've got lipstick all over you, where are the—oh, hello, Mother, you remember Cade MacInnis, don't you?"

Lori's lipstick was bright pink. Scrubbing at his mouth with the back of his left hand, subduing the urge to laugh, Cade said formally, if not entirely truthfully, "I'm delighted to see you again, Mrs. Campbell," and held out his other hand.

Marion Campbell's hair was rigidly coiffed, her makeup restrained and her dress an unexceptional beige; this was all much as Cade would have expected. Yet there was something different about her. The firmness of her handshake? Her candid appraisal of him? Or even the fact that she was standing in her daughter's kitchen against the express wishes of her husband?

She said, "Hello, Cade. I'd have known you anywhere, and yet you've changed."

"I'd have said exactly the same of you, Marion."

His reply was, in its way, a challenge. We meet in Lori's kitchen on an even footing, is what Cade was saying. I'm no longer your husband's hired hand.

"Then we're both to be commended," Marion Campbell said dryly. "Lori tells me you're a partner in Sam Withrod's garage—Morris takes the Rover there."

"Then I'll look forward to seeing him, too," Cade said with a gleam of devilment in his eye.

Lori said hastily, "Mother brought a bottle of wine, Cade, would you mind opening it for me?"

"A pleasure," Cade said, and decided that if he wasn't to make love to Lori this evening, he was at least going to ensure Marion got the message he was very much part of her daughter's life. He settled down to enjoy himself, and was rewarded an hour later by having Lori hiss in his ear, "You're really turning on the charm, aren't you?"

He was carving the roast and Marion was in the bedroom with the girls. Putting down the knife and fork, he ran his hands down her body with lingering pleasure. "Just want to make sure she knows what the score is," he drawled.

"Do you know what she told me?" Lori said. "That she always liked you. That she thought you were a fine young man who appreciated the work ethic. And that if she'd been twenty years younger, she'd have been after you herself. My own *mother!*"

Lori looked so scandalized that Cade started to laugh. She said crossly, "You have a warped sense of humor."

Cade picked up his glass of red wine, savoring it on his tongue; it was the best he'd ever drunk. From behind him a small voice said, "Is that what your daddy used to drink?"

For a moment Cade was knocked off balance; with searing clarity he remembered discovering Dan MacInnis's stash of cheap gin behind the tool chest in the garage. He'd been about seven at the time. Lori said, "Liddy, you shouldn't—"

"It's okay," Cade said. "He'd drink pretty well anything he could get his hands on, Liddy. It was sort of like a disease."

"D'you have it, too?"

"No, I don't."

The look in her eyes wasn't so much hostile as unfathomable. Wishing he knew what she was thinking, Cade said, "You can ask me whatever you want, Liddy, I hope you know that."

She shifted her feet. "Can I have more pop, Mum?"

End of conversation, thought Cade, and picked up the knife. Even though Liddy didn't speak to him again all evening, he was still heartened. He left fairly early, went home to his clean apartment and watched television until he was tired enough to sleep in the freshly laundered sheets.

On Monday he fixed the Alfa Romeo and on Monday evening went through his procedure step by step with Sam. On Tuesday Lori invited him for dinner again; her mother was leaving on the bus the next morning. Cade liked Marion. But she couldn't leave soon enough for him.

He was pouring the wine, Marion was helping Liddy cut her meat and Lori serving the gravy when the buzzer rang. Puzzled, Lori said, "Who could that be? It's a funny time of day for visitors."

When she pushed the button, a man's voice snarled over the intercom. Lori gave a startled gasp. Pressing the lock release, she faltered, "Come on up, Dad."

Marion said, "Oh my goodness. It's Morris."

Rachel said, "Gramps? What's he doing here?"

Liddy said nothing. Neither did Cade. With a kind of unholy amusement he sat back in his chair to await events. With himself, Lori, Marion and Morris in the same room, he was quite sure these events wouldn't be dull.

CHAPTER TWELVE

WHEN Lori opened the door, she said politely, "Dad, I'm—"

Her father pushed past her. Cade surged to his feet. Morris Campbell was the same bullheaded, red-faced dictator he'd always been, he thought. No changes there.

Morris didn't even see Cade; all his attention was on his wife. "Marion, you'll come home with me right this minute. And you won't be back."

Cade stood still, ready to intervene if necessary. Marion put down her napkin. Although her fingers were shaking slightly, she said steadfastly, "Morris, when Lori left Ray and you cut her out of our lives, you went too far."

"So you've been deceiving me for months!"

"I will not allow you to rob me of my granddaughters and my daughter."

It was open rebellion. Lori sucked in her breath. Rachel and Liddy watched in a fascinated silence as Morris's face got redder and redder. Marion added, "Rachel and Liddy are right here in front of you, Morris. Haven't they both grown in the last year?"

Morris looked from one to the other of the girls. Rachel piped, "Hi, Gramps. I play soccer now."

Liddy scowled at him. "Don't you be mad at my nanny."

Morris blustered, "Young lady, I will not tolerate—"

Ruthlessly Lori interrupted him. "You be quiet for a minute, Dad. It's my turn. Ten years ago you paid three hoodlums to attack Cade MacInnis. To beat him up. That was an absolutely unforgivable thing to do."

Lightly rocking back and forth on the balls of his feet, Cade drawled, "Hello, Mr. Campbell."

For the first time Morris looked his way. The older man's jaw dropped. With only a remnant of his former bravado he said, "MacInnis...what are you doing here?"

"Dating Lori," Cade said, and put a proprietary arm around her shoulders to make sure Morris got the message.

But Morris had visibly wilted. Into the silence Marion said, "So you see, Morris, there've been a lot of changes. Part of being a good businessman is maintaining flexibility in the face of change, isn't that what you're always telling me? Lori, why don't you get another chair, dear? The roast is delicious, Morris, and I took two bottles of wine out of the cellar, I do hope I chose a good vintage."

Morris looked at the label and paled. "Oh yes," he said in a hollow voice, "a very good vintage. The very best, in fact."

"Good," said Marion. "This reunion deserves the best, doesn't it?" Her hands were steady now; but her eyes met her husband's in open pleading.

For a moment it hung on the balance. Then Cade put a clean glass on the table and filled it with wine and Lori brought in a chair. Morris cleared his throat. He picked up the glass and said with something of his normal bluffness, "To reunions. To my daughter and her family. And—" he looked over at Cade "—to old acquaintances."

Everyone clinked their glasses. Morris sat down, savoring the wine, a look of exquisite pain on his face. "You've already drunk the other bottle?"

"On Monday," Marion said cheerfully, filling a plate for him. "How did you know where to find me, Morris?"

"I got home a day early. I looked in your address book when Meakins said you'd taken the bus to Halifax. I drove up in the Rover."

"I was telling Cade you take it to Sam's garage. Cade is a partner there now."

"A partner, eh? Now that's a good little business."

"Very good," Cade said. "Eventually I'll be full owner."

"You always were a hard worker," Morris said.

Rachel said eagerly, "Does this mean we can come back to your house now, Gramps, and play in the attic?"

"Yes, Rachel," he said, cutting into his roast beef. "Perhaps this very weekend."

"How lovely," Marion said. "Thank you, Morris." She smiled at him as proudly and happily as a young bride.

Morris cleared his throat again. "Past time," he said gruffly and patted his wife's hand.

It was as near to an apology as they were likely to get, thought Cade; yet he had to concede Morris was being surprisingly gracious in defeat. The conversation became more general and the wine bottle was drained to the last drop. Lori produced a chocolate cream pie and coffee and Liddy hauled Marvin into the kitchen to show her grandfather. Eventually Lori and Morris put the girls to bed while Marion and Cade washed the dishes. Then Morris said heartily, "Lori, Marion and I would be very happy if you and the girls would come to Juniper Hills this weekend."

"Saturday afternoon we could, after Rachel's soccer game. Providing Cade can come."

Manfully Morris said, "Delighted, of course."

"He can drive us in his Mercedes," Lori said naughtily.

Five minutes later she had closed the door behind her mother and father. She sank down on the nearest chair.

"My head's spinning," she said. "You go along thinking you know your parents, and then something happens
and you realize you don't know them at all. Mum was
magnificent. And so, in his own way, was Dad.
Astounding!"

"Your dad's missed all three of you and was too darn
stubborn to admit it. What's your sitter's phone number?"

"Sitter?" she repeated.

He passed her the receiver. "We need to celebrate.
Where better than in bed?"

"You do go for the essentials, Cade," Lori said ed-
gily.

"You've got a problem with that?"

"The shortest distance between two points isn't necessarily the best route."

He scowled at her. "I don't have any idea what you're
talking about."

"No, you don't, do you?" she said with a brilliant
smile, punching the seven digits with more energy than
was necessary. She then spoke to someone called Bev
and passed the phone back to Cade. "She'll be here in
ten minutes...I'm going to have a shower."

What had that been about? Was the man born who
could understand what was going on inside a woman?
More specifically, would he, Cade, ever understand
Lori? Perhaps it would come with practice, he thought.
How else could he fathom, for instance, that brilliant
smile that hadn't quite reached her eyes?

Twenty minutes later Cade was ushering Lori into his
apartment, which, because he hadn't spent much time
there, was still commendably clean and tidy. Taking her
by the hand, he led her straight to his bedroom; the head-
board of the bed was antique oak, the carpet Turkish and
the bedspread figured Indian cotton.

"Well, here we are," Lori said with that same edge to her voice.

Cade had had enough. "Do you or do you not want to go to bed with me?"

She tossed her head; her eyes glittered like jewels. "Actually, I feel lewd, lustful and lascivious."

But not loving.

Luckily Cade hadn't spoken those words out loud. He pulled her sweater over her head and said, not altogether joking, "Sometimes you talk too much."

"Whereas you don't talk—"

Cade closed her mouth with his own and unclasped her bra, seeking out her breasts with all the urgency of a man who had thought of very little else for the last three nights. He felt her quiver like an overstrung bow; as he fell on top of her on the bed, she tugged at his shirt and thrust her hands against his hair-roughened skin. He muttered, "What were you saying?"

"Nothing," Lori said faintly, "nothing at all."

"Good," said Cade and proceeded to do his level best to drive her completely out of control. He must have succeeded; their climax was mutual, fast and fierce. When he could talk, he said with a smothered laugh, "Darling Lori, I was like Marvin attacking his feed bowl."

"Are you comparing me to canned cat food?"

"Gourmet Dinner." He rested his face on her breast, listening to the staccato beat of her heart with huge delight. "Give me five minutes. Then we should try for a little more complexity...more like your dad's wine."

She giggled. "Poor Dad. He'd probably been saving that for years...Cade, do you know what he said to me while we were putting the girls to bed? I still can hardly believe it. Soon after Ray and I separated, he began to realize Ray had played him for a fool. A bunch of under-the-counter deals that basically took Dad to the cleaners.

Dad had been wanting to see me for months, but he was too stubborn to admit he'd made a mistake.''

"Three cheers for Marion.''

"You said it! But that's not all.'' Lori ran her finger lightly down Cade's chest. "I do love the way your muscles contract when I do that, it's very sexy…where was I?''

"Your dad,'' Cade said, straight-faced.

"Oh yes. The reason he hired those three thugs was because, in a perverted sort of way, he respected you so much. He knew it was no good just to talk to you. He did say he'd never done anything like that before or since.''

"I should be complimented?''

"Well, sort of.'' Her brow furrowed. "I think he was really sorry. I'm not sure he can actually say so.''

"I'll be a guest in his house this weekend—that's not a bad apology.''

"I'm so happy about what happened this evening, Cade—all of us together again. The girls need their grandparents, and I've missed being able to go home…but, you know, all of us are better for the break. I was so proud of Mum. And of Dad, too.''

Cade pulled her close, rocking her in his arms. "It'll make your life a lot easier, too,'' he said, and wondered if that would mean she wouldn't need him anymore.

"Oh, I'm not moving back,'' she said swiftly. "I like my independence too much for that.''

This didn't exactly reassure Cade. But why should he fret about the future when the present held the silken slide of Lori's thigh alongside his leg, the softness of her breast against his rib cage? He muttered, "We're talking too much again,'' and set about demonstrating to her his appreciation of the bouquet, texture and flavor of the finest of wines.

She was more than willing to be appreciated.

He could get addicted to making love to Lori. Or was he already?

The next evening at twenty to nine Lori phoned Cade; they'd agreed to go to a late movie after the girls were in bed. Cade said, making no effort to mask how eager he was to see her, "I can pick you up in five minutes."

She said raggedly, "I can't go, Cade, I'm sorry."

His hand clenched around the receiver. "Why not?"

"We were having supper and Rachel said something about Ray and suddenly it seemed like the right time to talk to Liddy about him. I've been putting it off, I know I have, waiting for the perfect moment. I'd given it a lot of thought and I did the very best I could to be gentle with her as well as honest. But she didn't take it very well. She got angry at first. Then she went all quiet." Lori's voice shook. "She's asleep now. But I think I should stay home in case she wakes, or has a bad dream."

Desperate to comfort her, Cade said, "I'll come over."

"No! No, you mustn't."

Feeling as though all six men in the alleyway had kicked him in the ribs, Cade barked, "Why can't I, Lori?"

"It'll complicate things if she wakes up."

He hated being seen as a complication; hated being banished from the stage when he was one of the players. Or was he just a bit player? Is that what she was implying? "And what about you?" he demanded.

"Me? What do you mean?"

"Seems like I'm complicating your life more than Liddy's. Are you telling me to back off?"

There was an instant of total silence. Then Lori said, "I—no, of course not."

She sounded utterly unconvincing; the pain in Cade's

chest congealed to the hardness of ice. He tried to breathe through it, to think rationally, and failed on both counts.

"Cade…are you still there?"

Struggling to grasp the commonplace, he said, "Will you send her to school tomorrow?"

"I think so. Try and keep everything as normal as possible. I just *wish* I'd told her what was going on at the time."

So did Cade. But he didn't say so. What was the point? What was the point of anything if Lori only saw him as a complication? Knowing he couldn't take any more of this, he said tightly, "I'm going out for a run—I'll talk to you tomorrow," and without giving her the chance to reply dropped the receiver into its cradle.

Quickly he changed into his running gear, stretched out his calf muscles against the side of the house and set out at a fast clip through the dark streets of the city. The leaves were falling, and there was an autumn chill to the air; filled with foreboding, Cade circled the Commons, where the fountains splashed their tall, ethereal plumes.

What would he do if Lori banished him from her life? He'd lose all three of them. But by far the worst would be losing Lori.

Maybe he already had.

The prospect was unbearable. I can't lose her, Cade thought with icy clarity, I can't!

He stumbled over a grass verge and hastily recovered his balance. What the hell was going on here? If he couldn't bear to lose her, did that mean he was in love with her?

His steps slowed. In love with Lori? Of course he was. He'd fallen in love with her when he was twenty and he'd never stopped loving her; after that scene at the garage he'd called it hatred instead, and left town as soon as he could. For nine years as he'd circled the globe he'd buried her deep in his psyche, getting on with his life and keeping his distance from women. And then he'd come home.

Lori was the reason he'd come home. Lori *was* home.

What a jerk you are, MacInnis! Took you one heck of a long time to figure out what's been going on.

He picked up speed, doing another circuit of the Commons, feeling as though he could run all night. He loved Lori. A woman whose body entranced him, whose adventurous spirit called to his own, and whose laughter and tears were woven into the very fabric of his life.

Whose daughters he loved, too.

Rachel and Liddy, one so artless and forthcoming, the other as stubborn as her own grandfather. He, Cade, would like to be their father, to live with them every day and watch them grow toward womanhood.

He wanted to marry their mother.

Marry her, live with her, sleep with her…maybe even have another child with her. Grinning like an idiot, Cade started his third circuit of the Commons. He'd like to father a child. Lori's child. He'd like that a lot.

For a man who called himself a loner, he'd come a long way. Which had nothing to do with the miles he'd covered since Lori had phoned him this evening.

The loose gravel crunched beneath his sneakers and Cade's euphoria suddenly collapsed. That phone call. Had Lori's hesitation meant she did want him to back off? That she couldn't tolerate the conflict between her younger daughter and her lover? That she didn't love him?

She loved going to bed with him, he knew that. She adored his body and enjoyed his company. He knew that, too. But he didn't have a clue whether she felt anything deeper and more lasting toward him. Not a clue.

If he asked her to marry him, would she accept? Or would she turn him down flat?

She'd turn him down. He was certain of it.

Cade labored on, his legs like lead weights. He was trapped in Halifax because of his partnership with Sam and his house in French Bay...he couldn't take off around the world a second time to escape from Lori. He'd have to stay put, working in the city where she lived, meeting her by chance, being constantly reminded of all he'd lost.

His heart felt as though it were being squeezed by a steel fist, his body as though he'd run twenty miles. Desperately he groped for even a glimmer of hope in the midst of his soul's darkness. What if he waited, bided his time? Maybe, just maybe, Lori would grow to love him.

He hated waiting; patience wasn't one of his virtues. What he wanted to do was rush to Lori's apartment this minute and propose to her. End the suspense.

Shoot yourself in the foot, why don't you?

You've got to wait. And not just for Lori; for Liddy, too. You need Liddy to accept you and Lori to love you.

You don't want much, do you?

Cade didn't do a fourth circuit of the Commons; he went home and had a shower instead. Lori hadn't left any messages on his machine, and he lacked the courage to phone her either that night or early the next morning before he left for work. He'd never thought of himself as a coward. But then, when had the stakes been so high?

The garage, fortunately, was busy enough to keep him more than occupied. He and Miguel were replacing the brake shoes on a Mazda when Joel called him to the phone. It must be Sam; or the supplier in Toronto. It wouldn't be Lori. His mouth dry, Cade picked up the receiver and said hello.

"It's Lori. Liddy's run away."

Although her voice was dead calm, Cade wasn't deceived. "Did she go to school?" he rapped.

"Yes. Rachel left her in the playground. But I decided I should call her teacher to explain that Liddy might not be herself this morning, and that's when I found out she was absent. Cade, what'll I do?"

"Have you phoned the police?"

"No. I wanted to talk to you first."

Even in the grip of a cold fear he was deeply gratified that she'd turned to him for help. "Does she have any money?"

"I checked. Her piggybank's gone. She had about twenty dollars in it."

His brain ranged over various options, trying to picture what Liddy might do. "The bus," he said. "Your mother came to Halifax on the bus. Would she have gone to her grandparents?"

"Maybe." Lori's voice shook. "Or she might try and find her father, she wouldn't have any concept of how far away Texas is."

"I'll take a run to the bus depot right now...it's not that far from the school, I wouldn't be surprised if that's where she's gone. If I don't get anywhere there, I'll go to the train station. But if she hasn't been seen in either place, we'll have to call the police. They can question the kids at school and put out an alert. Hang in there, Lori."

"Phone me as soon as you can, won't you? I'm desperate to be out searching, but I know I've got to stay home in case she comes back."

He wanted to say, *I love you.* But he was quite sure she wouldn't hear him. He said goodbye, told Miguel what had happened and shucked off his overalls. Ten minutes later he parked outside the bus station.

As Cade pushed open the glass door of the waiting

room, he saw a little girl shrink down in her seat. It was Liddy. His first emotion was a relief so overwhelming that his knees felt weak; he was already beginning to understand that becoming a parent made one vulnerable to the most terrible of losses. His second emotion was uncertainty. Now what? He'd been so intent on finding Liddy, he hadn't thought what he was going to say to her when he did.

He crossed the tiled floor. Sitting down beside her, he said quietly, "Running away usually doesn't fix things, Liddy. And your mum's really worried about you. How about if you and I get some hot chocolate and a couple of doughnuts and try and talk about what's happened?"

Liddy nodded; she was perilously close to tears.

Cade took her hand and walked to the nearest snack bar with her; her palm was very small in his, and also very cold. He let her take her time picking out the kind of doughnut she wanted, phoning Lori in the meantime to tell her he'd found Liddy; then he led her to a table by the window. He took a bite of his Boston cream and chewed it slowly, wondering where he should begin. Liddy burst out, "Aren't you going to tell me off?"

"No. That's your mother's job."

Liddy's little blue eyes filled with tears. "I ran away 'cause she said my daddy hit her and I didn't b'lieve her. I was going to ask Nanny if it was true."

Praying for wisdom, Cade said, "It is true, Liddy. He wanted to be married to someone else, and he didn't always behave very well...have you ever seen a kid throw a tantrum?"

Liddy brightened a little. "Kenny Stone, he yelled and screamed at the teacher in art class."

"Well, even though grown-ups aren't supposed to have tantrums, I think your dad threw a couple. And because he's a big man, he hurt your mum."

"Kenny Stone broke a chair."

"Your dad could have done a lot of damage to your mother. She was right to leave, Liddy—she had to."

Liddy poked her finger into her doughnut. "She had a bruise on her face one day 'n' told me she fell off a ladder. But that was a lie."

"She didn't tell you the truth right away because she didn't want to upset you. Until you were old enough to understand."

Liddy excavated a bigger hole. "He didn't send me a birthday card. Did your dad forget your birthday ever?"

"Yes, he did," Cade admitted. "When I was seven and again when I was nine. I was a boy, so I thought I wasn't supposed to cry. But it sure hurt."

"Are you going to marry my mum?"

Cade stopped with his doughnut halfway to his mouth. He put it back on his plate and looked straight at her; surely she deserved the truth. "I'd like to very much. But I haven't known her very long so I haven't asked her yet, and I don't know whether she'll say yes or no." He paused. "When I ask her, I'll let you know what she says. But for now, can this be our secret?"

"I like secrets," Liddy said. "Specially ones Rachel doesn't know about."

Parenthood, Cade could see, could be fraught with pitfalls other than the terror of loss. More mundane pitfalls, like sibling rivalry. "Drink up, sweetie," he said.

Liddy was still pushing her doughnut around her plate. "If you marry my mum, would we live in your house, the one she told us about?"

"I guess so."

"I'd like that. I'd like to be by the sea." Liddy gave him a sudden, cherubic smile that was like sunshine after rain, and took a big gulp of hot chocolate. Some of it dribbled down her chin. Cade reached over and wiped it off. This small gesture, so ordinary, seemed momentous to him. Was it his way of putting his seal on Liddy, as in his bed he had claimed her mother?

If he loved Lori, he also loved her children. Both of them.

He had no idea what he'd do if—or when—Lori said no.

He couldn't throw a tantrum, he thought wryly, and drained his mug. That course of action was out.

He and Liddy drove back to Lori's apartment. Liddy talked the whole way, telling him about her teacher and how Kenny Stone and two other boys had taken her schoolbag one day and thrown it in a puddle. "I kicked him," she said with great satisfaction. "Did you take girls' book bags?"

"I probably did. Boys can be like that."

"I hate Kenny Stone." She looked at Cade sideways. "But I don't hate you anymore."

He grinned at her from ear to ear. "I'm glad," he said.

When they arrived, Lori was waiting out in the hallway. She threw her arms around her daughter and burst into tears. Liddy started to cry, too. Cade went into the kitchen, found a box of tissues and accepted Lori's incoherent thanks and a bone-cracking hug that he was sure had everything to do with gratitude and nothing to do with love. He then caught sight of the clock on the stove. "I've got to get back to work," he said, and knew that once again he was being an arrant coward. Liddy had accepted him, so that hurdle was past. Which left only one final hurdle: what Lori felt—or didn't feel—toward him. A hurdle as high as the bridges that spanned the harbor. "I'll talk to you tonight," he added hurriedly. "'Bye, Liddy."

Liddy gave him a hug every bit as fervent as her mother's and Cade made his escape. At the garage two breakdowns had been added to the day's roster, and the hospital had phoned to say Sam could go home late in the afternoon; Cade had offered to stay with Sam that first night. So Cade spent the evening scrubbing various grimy and greasy surfaces in Sam's kitchen rather than dealing with the chaos in his emotional life; although he did talk to Lori on the phone.

She was, she said, very grateful for his help and she wondered if she could borrow his car the next day. "My noon-hour class is canceled and I need to sit by the shore and watch the waves before we go away for the weekend," she said. "Too much has happened too fast, I'm reeling from it all."

Cade recognized the feeling only too well. "Of course you can. I'll leave it outside your apartment on my way to work."

"How's Sam?"

"Sam's fine. Sam's kitchen, however, needs a passel of industrial cleaners with buckets of lye and very strong stomachs."

She chuckled. "Poor Cade...why don't I cook supper for you tomorrow evening?"

"Thanks, I'd like that," he said, and when they rang off, went back to scrubbing the counter with disinfectant.

He was beginning to hate the phone. He wanted the real woman instead. In his arms, in his house, in his life. For the rest of his life.

Patience, Cade. Patience.

CHAPTER THIRTEEN

AT TEN to four on Friday afternoon Joel again called Cade to the phone. "Cade MacInnis," he said.

There was a tiny silence. "Cade? This is Rachel. Mum's not home. Do you know where she is?"

"Not home?" he repeated stupidly.

"She's always here when we get home from school. I used my key to get in, but we don't know where she is."

Rachel was doing her best to be the competent elder sister; but Cade could hear the anxiety in her voice. "She borrowed my car to go out to the shore. But she should have been back by now," he said, thinking aloud. "She didn't leave a note?"

"No. She's never been gone like this."

Car accident, he thought sickly, and shoved the nightmare images to the back of his mind. "Rachel, give me your sitter's number and I'll arrange for her to go to your place. Then I'll phone you back. If your mum's still not home, I'll go out to my house and look for her."

"That's good," said Rachel.

Luckily Bev could go to the apartment right away; when he checked, Lori still wasn't home. Cade grabbed the garage's cellular phone, borrowed Sam's car and took off. It was Friday afternoon; the traffic was clogged and his heart seemed to be trapped in his throat. Lori, he knew, would never willingly be late for her daughters. Something was wrong.

As he crept around the rotary he dialed the hospital; no one by the name of Lori Cartwright had been admitted to emergency. The double line of traffic crawled up the hill, Cade keeping his eyes trained for Lori in his Mercedes. He phoned her apartment again. Bev, sounding capable and calm, told him Lori had neither phoned nor come home. The traffic gradually picked up momentum. It started to rain. It wasn't until then that something that had been nagging at Cade's mind came to the surface: the wind.

The treetops were bowing to the wind, stray yellow leaves dipping and swirling above the cars; a crow, wind-driven, skitted across his vision. Candy wrappers danced in the gutters.

Lori hated wind. Was afraid of it.

What in heaven's name had happened to her?

If Cade had needed proof that he loved Lori, he got it in that drive to French Bay. By the time the highway dipped to the shoreline and he saw foam streaking the water and waves rearing against the rocks, his chest was knotted with fear and his shoulders tight with tension. By now the rain was pelting on the windshield; he'd be willing to bet, if Lori had set out this morning, that she didn't have a raincoat.

The drenched spruce trees along the driveway had been whipped to a frenzy. His car was parked outside the house, which was locked and deserted.

The shore. She'd said she needed to sit by the shore.

Cade grabbed his oilskins from the back porch and ran down the field toward the rocks, his cheeks stinging from the cold rain, his ears filled with the roar of the sea's assault. "Lori!" he called. "Lori…"

He staggered around the little promontory that edged the cove. The sand beach had disappeared beneath the marbled foam, strands of seaweed flung up into the grass. Because the tide was as high as he'd ever seen it, the island seemed to have shrunk. Waves leaped above the granite boulders that connected it to the beach.

He shouted Lori's name again, his only answer the

screams of the herring gulls who were hanging on the wind with lazy, white-winged elegance. She couldn't have drowned, he thought in sheer terror, and knew that subconsciously he'd been searching the seething waters for a fuschia-colored sweater.

"Lori!" he yelled at the top of his lungs.

His head jerked to the left. Was that a voice?

And then he saw her, crouched under the shelter of the shrub spruce on the leeward side of the island. Even as he watched, she began pushing through the branches, staggering against the gale as she headed for the causeway. He shouted her name again, hearing the wind throw it back at him, and started running toward the island. Then Lori waved at him, and through the rain and spray Cade caught the gleam of her smile.

His relief was so intense that for a moment his knees buckled. First Liddy, now Lori. He was discovering the cost to love, a cost he'd never really understand until the last few days. Being a loner was safe. But he wasn't a loner anymore.

He loved Lori with all his heart. He had to tell her so. Today. It couldn't wait any longer, and if she didn't love him back, at least he'd have been honest about his feelings.

Being the strong, silent type wasn't working anymore.

If she didn't love him, *he* might as well maroon himself on the island. For good.

He'd reached the causeway. Although the slam of waves and the hiss of spray were awe-inspiring, the rocks were deflecting most of the sea's wrath; he knew he could make it over to the island, although he wasn't so sure he'd be able to coax Lori back. Picking out his route, he stepped into the water.

Cade was soaked to the thighs before he'd taken more than a few steps; cold bit into his flesh. Bending his head against the spray, he gripped the ledges with his left hand, his feet seeking out the shoals and sandbars. The kelp was slippery as ice; twice he stumbled and almost fell. But foot by slow foot he was getting closer to the island. Closer to Lori.

Thank God he'd spent all those hours at the gym.

His hair was plastered to his forehead; rain and salt spray ran in rivulets down his cheeks, streaming down his yellow oilskins. Seizing the rough granite edges of the last heap of boulders, Cade hauled himself up on land, his heart thrumming in his chest, his jeans clinging to his calves.

Lori flew out of the trees and threw herself at him. "Are you all right?" she cried. "I was so worried about you, I thought you might drown right there in front of me, oh Cade, I'm so glad to see you." She drew a jagged breath. "The girls—are they home?"

"Bev's with them." He shucked off his jacket and put it around her. "As soon as we get back to the house we'll call them on the cell phone."

"I can't go across there," she gasped. "That's why I'm here. Because I was too afraid to go back on my own. I was doing a lot of thinking and not paying any attention and then for a while I dozed off…it wasn't until I woke up I realized the wind and the tide had come up and it was too late."

She was talking very fast and her eyes were huge blue pools in a face as white as foam. "You can go across," Cade said. "With me."

"It's the wind, you know how I've always hated it."

How could she live with him in his house by the sea if she hated wind? "You'll be all right with me…you've got to trust me, that's all."

Lori looked across the narrow little causeway. "That's a lot," she said with some of her normal spirit.

"Yes," said Cade with an air of discovery, "it is."

She was now scowling at him. He liked that a lot

better than white-faced fear. "If we're going to do this," she said, "let's do it. You go first."

He took her hand in his. "Hold on to the rocks with your other hand and put your feet where I put mine."

As they stepped back into the water, the full violence of the gale struck them. Over his shoulder Cade saw Lori flinch and shrink back. With all the force of his will he shouted, "You're safe with me, Lori. And you can do it, I know you can."

As she gripped her lower lip in her teeth and took another step forward, Cade wondered if he'd ever loved her as much as he did right now. Courage and trust: a fine basis for marriage, he thought, and reached out for the first rough-edged boulder.

Step by step they fought against the wind and rain and the pellets of spray. He kept up a constant stream of encouragement, and halfway across, his feet anchored firmly on a shoal, he kissed her salty lips. "You're doing fine...I'm proud of you."

"There's a time and place for romance and this ain't it," Lori announced; but laughter glinted in her eyes.

She's forgotten about the wind, he thought, ducking a hail of spray. "You mean you won't make love with me here? It would be an elemental experience, you've got to admit that."

"I will not!"

He laughed, gripped her cold hand tighter in his and stepped into deeper water. Three or four minutes later they reached the shore. "Let's run," he said, "it'll warm you up."

Hand in hand, they raced up the grassy slope to the house. Cade opened the door and they fell inside. "Towels in the upstairs bathroom," he gasped. "I'll get you some dry clothes, I keep a few things here. And I'll turn up the heat."

Fifteen minutes later they were both sitting on the

futon in his bedroom drinking mugs of tea, Lori arrayed in sweatpants and a big flannel shirt of Cade's, Cade in a pair of old cords and a T-shirt. They'd phoned home. He'd dried her hair and his own. There was nothing else to do but tell her the words that had been burning his tongue ever since his late-night jog around the Commons.

It took a lot more courage to do that than any crossing of the causeway, no matter how high the tide.

He said, and because he was nervous he sounded curt, "Lori, I've got to be honest with you. Up front. I can't go on the way we are, it's—"

She interrupted him, looking far more terrified than she had on the island. "Cade, you don't have to say it. Really you don't."

"That's where you're wrong!"

She lifted a hand to ward him off. "Please…I know you don't love me, even though I wish you did because I'm in love with you. I've probably loved you for years, ever since that night I was sixteen and you saw me in my first evening dress. But you were always so serious and remote, and at the time I don't think I really understood what I was feeling. Besides, Dad kept throwing me together with Ray. But then I tried to seduce you—I shouldn't have, I see that now, but I was only eighteen and until I kissed you I didn't have a clue what sexual desire was all about—and you rejected me. With the best of intentions, I'm sure, but it hurt horribly and afterward I behaved really badly just to top it all off."

She took a frantic breath, shaking her head as he started to speak. "Let me finish and then I'll shut up, I swear I will. The reason I was so frightened when we bumped into each other at the gym was because I'd never forgotten what kissing you felt like—it was never like that with Ray—and when you put your arms around me I could have been eighteen all over again…oh God,

I've got to stop this." Her voice a thin thread, she blurted, "Cade, I don't think I can go on with our affair. You don't love me, you see, and it all hurts too much."

She clutched her mug and took a big swallow of tea. Cade said blankly, "Why do you think I don't love you?"

"You said so. In my kitchen that evening after we'd gone to bed together for the first time. You told Rachel we weren't in love with each other, we were just friends. Under some circumstances friends is a fine word, but not when we'd just made love in a way I'd never experienced before. Made *love*. You also said it was inappropriate to talk about the future. Inappropriate! Yuk." She tossed her tangled curls, her chin raised defiantly. "Don't misunderstand me, I was certainly interested in taking you back to bed. But not if that's all there was to it. A roll in the futon."

"Lori, I was trying to keep my cool that evening. Making love with you had knocked me off my feet. I couldn't cope with the present, let alone the future."

"You expect me to believe that?"

"I didn't know what I was feeling!"

"That's not the message I got."

Her flood of words was finally starting to penetrate Cade's confusion. "When we collided with each other at the gym and I could have made love to you right there in the corridor, you were feeling the same way?"

"Oh yes. It was one more reason I did my best to keep you at a distance."

He digested this in silence; then, finally, he voiced that other, startling piece of information. "You're in love with me," he said.

"Yes." She gave him a very unloving look. "But don't let it go to your head. No doubt I'll get over it. By the time I'm ninety."

"Will you marry me?"

"Cade, don't play games!"

"I'm not! I've never done this before, and I can see I'm not doing it right...I'd better start over." Resting his hands on her shoulders, lost in the heavy fabric of his shirt, he kissed her with all the love in his heart.

She twisted away. "Don't! That's not fair, you know what it does to me."

"I'm trying to show you how much I love you. How I've never stopped loving you ever since I was twenty."

"*What?*"

"You heard. I've loved you since that very same night when you were sixteen...that evening dress has a lot to answer for. But you were Lorraine Campbell and I was plain Cade MacInnis with about as much hope of courting you as I had of keeping my dad sober. By the time I left Juniper Hills, I'd convinced myself I hated you. Even when we met in the gym, I still thought I did. But I was kidding myself. Royally."

She looked stunned. "You loved me way back then?"

Cade nodded. "But I never even suspected it."

"I made damn sure you didn't."

"And you still love me?"

"Yes," he said, adding with a crooked grin, "I love you and you love me. Do you think we should carry this to the next step and decide to get married?" His smile faded. "I want to marry you, Lori. More than I can say. I'm just sorry it's taken me so long to come to my senses."

Gaping at him, Lori said, "I'm wide awake and you're actually proposing to me."

"Yes or no?" Cade demanded, and waited for the answer on which his whole life depended.

"Yes. Oh yes." Her smile was as sudden and dazzling as sunlight piercing a cloud. "Nothing could make me happier."

"When?" he said.

She laughed, a cascade of pure joy. "You always go straight for the essentials, don't you? Tonight, tomorrow, as soon as we can, how's that for an honest answer?"

"I like it," he said, and kissed her again. "What about the girls?"

"Rachel will be ecstatic and Liddy's come around just amazingly, I know she'll be happy, too. Mum will think it's a fairy-tale ending and Dad will fuss and fume and be relieved I'm being looked after by a good man, which is something all women, according to him, need."

"But you don't," Cade said with a nasty sinking sensation in his belly. "You want to be independent."

"I did a lot of thinking about independence on the island." Her forehead crinkled. "Because I've been on my own for the last year, I know I can manage on my own. So I'm not marrying you out of fear or dependence—I'm marrying you because I want to."

"Not such a bad thing that the tide came up," he said.

"I don't think I'll ever be as afraid of the wind again, either."

Cade took her in his arms. "Liddy already knows I want to marry you, by the way. I told her the day I found her at the bus station."

"Well...she certainly knows how to keep a secret."

"It's taken you and me the better part of thirteen years to let a few secrets out. That we love each other, I mean."

"We'll do better in the next thirteen," she teased.

Gazing into the smudged blue of her eyes, so familiar and so beloved, Cade said, "I'm not good with words...although I'm getting better." His voice roughened. "I just want you to know that body and soul I'm yours until the day I die."

"I'm yours, too, dearest Cade," Lori said fervently.

Dearest Cade...through the lump in his throat Cade muttered, "Say that again."

"Dearest, darling and most adorable Cade, I love you, I lust after you, I'm enthralled and enraptured and bewitched by you." She gave him an impish smile. "How am I doing?"

"Enthralled and enraptured, huh?" he murmured, kissed her with lingering pleasure, and beneath her flannel shirt found the silken warmth of her belly and the soft weight of her breast. "Words are all very well, Lori Cartwright...but don't you think we should put them into action?"

Her answer was to pull him down on top of her. "If you think I look sexy in your shirt and pants, you've got it bad."

"I think you'll look a whole lot sexier without them," Cade said, and proceeded to put this more than satisfactorily to the test.

So it was another hour before they drove back into town. Cade paid Bev, who'd fed the girls their supper, and Bev left. Then he said, putting his arm around Lori and smiling at her daughters, "Your mum and I have something to tell you."

Lori said, "We're going to get married. Very soon."

Rachel's face lit up. "We'll all live together? And Cade'll be our father?"

"Yes and yes. We'll live in French Bay," her mother said.

"Their soccer team won the county championships last year," Rachel said with a big grin and threw herself at both of them.

Cade looked down at Liddy. Liddy said sedately, "That's nice. I'll like living by the sea. I always think that waves sound as though they're telling each other secrets." And she gave Cade an innocent smile.

Cade winked at her. He then said, "It's no secret that I love your mother more than I can say, Rachel and

Liddy...and that I'll do my very best to be a good father to both of you."

"Can we be bridesmaids?" Rachel asked.

"Absolutely," Lori said.

"I'll ask Sam to be my best man," Cade said. "He'll have to wear a suit, he won't like that."

"Will you wear a long white dress, Mum?" Liddy asked.

"I hope she will," Cade said, and in his eyes was the memory of their tumultuous lovemaking that afternoon, when he'd discovered the wonderful freedom of being able to tell Lori how much he loved her when her naked body was intimately pressed to his own. He'd never done that before. It warranted, at the very least, a long white dress.

As she blushed charmingly, he went on, "Your mother and I haven't had any supper yet. Why don't we all go out to a restaurant...I'm sure you could manage to force down an ice cream sundae." He suddenly grinned. "Do you know what I'd like you to do? All three of you? Wear the dungarees and shirts you were photographed in at the studio. Would you do that for me?"

So half an hour later, at the little Italian restaurant down the road, Cade was surrounded by his three blondes, all identically dressed and all looking very happy to be with him. He raised a glass of red wine inferior to Morris's but nevertheless palatable, and said, "To our family of four."

A family of four, he thought humbly, was an enormous gift for a man who'd always called himself a loner.

He'd never be a loner again. He raised his glass a second time. "To love," he said.

"To love," Lori echoed, and clinked her glass with his.

"Five," said Liddy. "You didn't count Marvin."

Head Down Under for twelve tales of heated romance in beautiful and untamed Australia!

**Here's a sneak preview of the first novel in
THE AUSTRALIANS**

Outback Heat **by Emma Darcy
available July 1998**

'HAVE I DONE something wrong?' Angie persisted, wishing Taylor would emit a sense of camaraderie instead of holding an impenetrable reserve.

'Not at all,' he assured her. 'I would say a lot of things right. You seem to be fitting into our little Outback community very well. I've heard only good things about you.'

'They're nice people,' she said sincerely. Only the Maguire family kept her shut out of their hearts.

'Yes,' he agreed. 'Though I appreciate it's taken considerable effort from you. It is a world away from what you're used to.'

The control Angie had been exerting over her feelings snapped. He wasn't as blatant as his aunt in his prejudice against her but she'd felt it coming through every word he'd spoken and she didn't deserve any of it.

'Don't judge me by your wife!'

His jaw jerked. A flicker of some dark emotion destroyed the steady power of his probing gaze.

'No two people are the same. If you don't know that, you're a man of very limited vision. So I come from the city as your wife did! That doesn't stop me from being an individual in my own right.'

She straightened up, proudly defiant, furiously angry with the situation. 'I'm *me*. Angie Cordell. And it's time you took the blinkers off your eyes, Taylor Maguire.'

Then she whirled away from him, too agitated by the explosive expulsion of her emotion to keep facing him.

The storm outside hadn't yet eased. There was nowhere to go. She stopped at the window, staring blindly at the torrential rain. The thundering on the roof was almost deafening but it wasn't as loud as the silence behind her.

'You want me to go, don't you? You've given me a month's respite and now you want me to leave and channel my energies somewhere else.'

'I didn't say that, Angie.'

'You were working your way around it.' Bitterness at his tactics spewed the suspicion. 'Do you have your first choice of governess waiting in the wings?'

'No. I said I'd give you a chance.'

'Have you?' She swung around to face him. 'Have you really, Taylor?'

He hadn't moved. He didn't move now except to make a gesture of appeasement. 'Angie, I was merely trying to ascertain how you felt.'

'Then let me tell you your cynicism was shining through every word.'

He frowned, shook his head. 'I didn't mean to hurt you.' The blue eyes fastened on hers with devastating sincerity. 'I truly did not come in here to take you down or suggest you leave.'

Her heart jiggled painfully. He might be speaking the truth but the judgements were still there, the judgements that ruled his attitude towards her, that kept her shut out of his life, denied any real sharing with him, denied his confidence and trust. She didn't know why it meant so much to her but it did. It did. And the need to fight for justice from him was as much a raging torrent inside her as the rain outside.

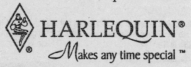

Take 4 bestselling love stories FREE

Plus get a FREE surprise gift!

Special Limited-time Offer

Mail to Harlequin Reader Service®

3010 Walden Avenue
P.O. Box 1867
Buffalo, N.Y. 14240-1867

YES! Please send me 4 free Harlequin Presents® novels and my free surprise gift. Then send me 6 brand-new novels every month, which I will receive months before they appear in bookstores. Bill me at the low price of $3.12 each plus 25¢ delivery and applicable sales tax, if any*. That's the complete price and a savings of over 10% off the cover prices—quite a bargain! I understand that accepting the books and gift places me under no obligation ever to buy any books. I can always return a shipment and cancel at any time. Even if I never buy another book from Harlequin, the 4 free books and the surprise gift are mine to keep forever.

106 HEN CE65

Name	(PLEASE PRINT)	
Address	Apt. No.	
City	State	Zip

This offer is limited to one order per household and not valid to present Harlequin Presents® subscribers. *Terms and prices are subject to change without notice. Sales tax applicable in N.Y.

UPRES-696   ©1990 Harlequin Enterprises Limited

Presents Extravaganza
25 YEARS!

**With the purchase of two Harlequin Presents®
books, you can send in for a FREE Silvertone Book
Pendant. Retail value $19.95. It's our gift to you!**

FREE SILVERTONE BOOK PENDANT

On the official proof-of-purchase coupon below, fill in your name,
address and zip or postal code, and send it, plus $1.50 U.S./
$2.50 CAN. for postage and handling, (check or money order—please
do not send cash), to Harlequin books: In the U.S.: 3010 Walden
Avenue, P.O. Box 9077, Buffalo, N.Y. 14269-9077; In Canada: P.O. Box
609, Fort Erie, Ontario L2A 5X3. Please allow 4-6 weeks for delivery.
Order your Silvertone Book Pendant now! Quantities are limited. Offer
for the FREE Silvertone Book Pendant expires December 31, 1998.

HP25POP

Coming Next Month

HARLEQUIN PRESENTS®

THE BEST HAS JUST GOTTEN BETTER!

#1965 FANTASY FOR TWO Penny Jordan
Mollie Barnes and Alex Villiers seemed to have nothing in
common. So why had she confessed her secret fantasy to
him? And why was it they couldn't seem to keep away from
each other?

#1966 THE DIAMOND BRIDE Carole Mortimer
(Nanny Wanted!)
Annie adored being Jessica Diamond's nanny, but her
relationship with Jessica's father was complicated! Rufus had
the power to make her laugh and cry—he also wanted to
make love to her! But Jessica had to come first....

#1967 RENDEZVOUS WITH REVENGE Miranda Lee
When Abby's boss, Ethan Grant, asked her to pose as his
lover at the conference, she knew that to him she was
probably just an expensive plaything. In fact, she turned out
to be a pawn in his game of revenge!

#1968 THE GROOM SAID MAYBE! Sandra Marton
(The Wedding of the Year)
It all began when Stephanie and David were seated next to
each other at a wedding. Stephanie needed a lawyer, and
David was one of the best, so she told him she needed
money. Then David confessed he needed a fiancée....

#1969 LONG-DISTANCE MARRIAGE Sharon Kendrick
Alessandra and Cameron married in haste, believing that
they could combine two careers in two different cities. But
with the pressure came problems, particularly when he
suggested that she leave work to have his baby....

#1970 LOVERS' LIES Daphne Clair
Joshua didn't recognize Felicia, but his obvious attraction to
her gave her the means to exact revenge for his betrayal of
her stepsister years ago. The problem was, Felicia herself
was not immune to his charms....